Cotswold Docs

Love is in the air at Clearbrook Medical Practice!

Welcome to the idyllic Cotswolds village of Clearbrook, famous for its rolling fields of lavender and quaint cheesecake shop. No wonder it has attracted three new GPs to its medical practice. And with new doctors breathing new life into the sleepy surgery, sparks soon begin to fly!
The surprise meeting of Lorna and Oliver triggers the rekindling of a decades-old bond, while single parents and new neighbors Bella and Max are drawn to each other from the moment they meet. But when crisis threatens, are any of them brave enough to take a chance on true love?

Find out in...

Lorna and Oliver's story
Best Friend to Husband?

Bella and Max's story
Finding a Family Next Door

Both available now

Dear Reader,

This book (and book one in the duet—
Best Friend to Husband?) deals with the implications
of long-term illness. Not just to the patient, but to
those around them—who live with them, care for
them and love them. Being a carer to your loved one
can be fulfilling and wonderful, but it can also cause
stress, exhaustion and a fear so great that it almost
becomes unbearable to live with. Carers walk a
difficult line and I wanted to explore a couple with a
lot on the line (being single parents to young children)
who must face the possibility of becoming a carer
(Max) and being the patient (Bella), especially as Max
has been a carer before and it broke him so much
that he swore to never do so again.

What do you do when the woman you have now
fallen in love with gets sick?

I hope you enjoy Bella and Max's story. They are
such wonderful characters and I had great fun writing
them.

Happy reading!

Louisa xxx

FINDING A FAMILY NEXT DOOR

LOUISA HEATON

MEDICAL ROMANCE

Harlequin®
MEDICAL ROMANCE

ISBN-13: 978-1-335-94287-6

Finding a Family Next Door

Harlequin Enterprises ULC
22 Adelaide St. West, 41st Floor
Toronto, Ontario M5H 4E3, Canada
www.Harlequin.com

Printed in U.S.A.

Louisa Heaton lives on Hayling Island, Hampshire, with her husband, four children and a small zoo. She has worked in various roles in the health industry—most recently four years as a community first responder, answering emergency calls. When not writing, Louisa enjoys other creative pursuits, including reading, quilting and patchwork—usually instead of the things she *ought* to be doing!

Books by Louisa Heaton

Harlequin Medical Romance

Christmas North and South

A Mistletoe Marriage Reunion

Cotswold Docs

Best Friend to Husband?

Greenbeck Village GPs

The Brooding Doc and the Single Mom
Second Chance for the Village Nurse

Night Shift in Barcelona

Their Marriage Worth Fighting For

Yorkshire Village Vets

Bound by Their Pregnancy Surprise

Single Mom's Alaskan Adventure
Finding Forever with the Firefighter
Resisting the Single Dad Surgeon

Visit the Author Profile page
at Harlequin.com for more titles.

To Nick, James, Becca, Jared and Jack x

**Praise for
Louisa Heaton**

"Another enjoyable medical romance from
Louisa Heaton with the drama coming courtesy of
life on a busy maternity ward. Lovely characters, a
great story, set in one of my favourite cities and an all
round easy engaging read."
—*Goodreads* on *Miracle Twins for the Midwife*

CHAPTER ONE

CLEARBROOK INFANTS' SCHOOL was situated down a small narrow lane and Bella could see that parking was a nightmare. She was glad that she had decided to walk Ewan in for his first day as everywhere she looked people were double parking, or patiently waiting, or even doing three-point turns when they realised there was nowhere to go. It was the first day back after the May half-term for most children, but the first day for Ewan, here at his new school.

It was a lovely day, the air filled with the scent of lavender from the fields all around. It was something that had surprised her when she'd come to Clearbrook for her own job interview. That rich, floral scent, the air so thick with it, it had almost made her feel sleepy. Even Priti, the practice manager, had joked that no one in Clearbrook suffered from insomnia.

The lavender helped some towards her nerves. Towards her headache. She was anxious for two reasons. It was her first day at Clearbrook Medical Practice as a new GP, but it was also Ewan's first day away from her for a whole day. Nine till three-thirty for school and then he was in the after-school club until six p.m. It was a heck of a long day. It had been him and her against the world for the last four years and, though she'd loved every moment of it with him, she couldn't wait to see what schooling would do to his character. What his favourite subjects would be. Who his friends would be. What he would want to be when he grew up.

Ewan was already good at reading. Bella had been reading to him since he was a baby and he already knew his alphabet and the ten times table. She'd been determined to raise a good boy, an educated, well-behaved, respectful boy, and the act of letting go and letting someone else teach him, someone else *influence* him, was terrifying.

But that was part of being a parent—letting go. Trusting in the system. Of course, she'd scanned the school OFSTED reports. Talked to the governors. Met the teachers. Ewan's first teacher was a lovely young woman called Miss Celic. She'd given off good vibes. Seemed warm and welcoming. Bella had been happy he was going into her class. She felt confident about it.

But she was still nervous. She had tried to prep Ewan for what would happen. Had even created a book for him, with photos of his school and his teacher that she'd copied from the school website. Shown him the playground and the corridors where he would hang his coat and bag, where he would go for his dinner and how to go to the after-school club when the bell rang at three-thirty and most of the other kids went home.

She knew what he would be eating—Monday was vegetable lasagne midday. The after-school club would give him toast and fruit to tide him over until he got home.

Bella knew he would be okay. He was a confident little boy—just as she'd raised him to be—but a tiny part of her, strangely, wanted him to resist going in. Part of her wanted him to cling to her and not let go when it was time to part and say goodbye.

As she entered the playground with the other parents, she could see a mass of children. Happy, playing. Some clinging to their parent's legs. She saw one guy standing alone, talking to his young daughter, who looked to be on the verge of tears. He was trying to calm her. Smiling. Soothing her. Wiping away her tears with a handkerchief. Was he a single dad? A stay-at-home dad? Maybe he had a job to go to after drop-off?

The little girl was beautiful. Hair a dark blonde, like her father's. Her eyes were large and blue. He was dressed for work. Dark trousers, a pale blue shirt, open at the neck. A suit jacket. He was handsome. Far too handsome, to be fair, and he probably knew it. The kind of man that could simply smile and easily schmooze you with his good looks and twinkling charm, bedazzling you with his beauty so much that it would be too late before you noticed the red flags of his behaviour.

She knew the type. Ewan's father had been like that and she refused to be pulled in by one ever again.

Mind you, she thought, *can't tar all guys with the same brush. Maybe this one's a unicorn?*

She imagined this handsome man prancing around in front of her, wearing hooves on his hands, a multicoloured tail swishing around behind him and a giant sparkling horn protruding from his head. Bella smiled to herself, then dismissed the image, far more interested in watching the guy be so tender and kind to his upset daughter. His face was the picture of patience and love and when he reached up to wipe away a tear from his daughter's face, she felt an ache.

Bella turned away from their private moment as the man then reached out to his daughter to give her a hug. 'Are you ready?' she asked Ewan, smiling, trying to look and sound confident with her decision to put him in for a full day straight away. The school had suggested that, until Ewan got used to the place, he only come part time for the first couple of days. Mornings only. Or afternoons only. But, as she'd explained to them, she couldn't do that with her job. Her job was full time and so she needed him in full time. She'd promised them that he would be fine, because she would prepare him for it. Ewan was strong, she'd told them. He'd be all right.

Ewan nodded, smiling.

He held her hand, but she could feel him trying to let go as he gazed at a group of boys playing on the playground equipment. There were rope bridges, a climbing frame, a slide, a circle of tyres, swings and what looked like a low climbing wall. The group of boys were having fun.

'Can I go and play, Mum?'

He'd be going in any minute and, though she wanted to stay every second she could with him before she'd have to let him go, she knew that he would need to make friends and so she nodded, reluctantly, and let him go. She watched him run away from her, without a care in the world as he joined the other boys. He seemed to seamlessly join in and was laughing and playing, clearly not worrying about her.

She felt a pang in her heart. Had she raised him to be *too* confident?

No. This is a good thing.

She was happy to know that she'd successfully raised him to be confident and outgoing—it was what she'd wanted. Being this way meant that he would cope with the long days apart from her and therefore it would make her life easier. She turned to look at all the other parents, her eyes falling again on the man, with his daughter, that she'd seen before. The man was standing now. He'd lifted his daughter into his arms and was hugging her, whispering soothing words into her ear. He was smiling. He kissed her ear and put her down again, the little girl slipping her hand into his and nodding to him, trying to be brave.

Part of her wanted that moment with Ewan. To give him one last moment of encouragement, one last pearl of wisdom that would make him feel brave enough to go into school without her. To have that experience that all the other parents talked about. But she wasn't going to get that and that was okay, too, because she would rather see him happy and smiling and enjoying himself than have him clinging to her leg and making her feel awful to leave him behind.

A whistle blew and the doors opened and teachers appeared.

Bella saw Miss Celic standing there in a pink summer dress and white bolero cardigan. She was greeting parents and children alike as they began to file past her towards their classroom and Bella turned to call for Ewan. To kiss him goodbye before he went in, but he was already past her, grabbing at his bag and lining up for his teacher.

She stood there, feeling proud of him for being so brave, so carefree. She'd wanted one last word to wish him good luck, but he was already gone. She laughed to herself instead. She was proud of a job well done. This was how she'd raised him to be. Confident. Brave. Outgoing. She'd raised a good boy and the evidence was there to see. She could go into work now and not worry about him.

Instead, she watched the man walk his daughter towards Miss Celic, saw him kneel, kiss his daughter's cheek one last time, saw him mouth the words *I love you* as his daughter gave him one last desperate hug. Miss Celic took the little girl's hand and led her wards into the school, the doors closing shut behind them, and then all the parents began to file away.

The man gave one last wave and blew a kiss, before his daughter disappeared from sight.

She knew he would remember this last moment. That memory that he would keep for ever now. Maybe something that he might bring up one day, say, at her wedding, talking of the moment he knew he had to let go of his daughter the first time, to make her own way in the world?

He disappeared into the migrating crowd of parents and she knew she had to get to work now. Had to face her own first day. It was a day that she'd been looking forward to for a long time.

This was the beginning of the fresh start. No more would she just be a locum GP, travelling here, there and everywhere to work the odd day, leaving Ewan behind with her own father, or with a childminder. No more would she face let downs and disappointments and be cheated of the chance to gain a long-term relationship with a set of patients.

Today, she began her role as a *permanent* member of staff at a surgery. A place where she could build relationships for the first time. A place where she would put down roots. Where she would raise her son to be a man. A good man. A strong man, who was respectful and kind and loving and loyal. She hoped to make good friends here, too.

It was a three-minute walk from the school to the medical centre. Not far. And what a beautiful walk it was. Down the lane, across the village green, a little way down the main street and there it was, on the left. Surrounded by old stone cottages, thatched rooves and gardens full of blooms. A fat ginger cat sat on top of the post box next door, surveying the green. She reached up to stroke it and the feline allowed it, head bumping into her hand with a loud purr.

'What's your name?' she asked, knowing she might sound silly, talking to a cat, but she loved cats and she'd promised Ewan they might get one, once they'd settled in properly. A rescue cat, maybe? Something older, that was just looking for someone's lap to sleep on every night?

And then she was there, standing outside the doors of Clearbrook Medical Practice, and she was straightening her clothes and checking her hair and sucking in a deep breath. The doors slid open at her approach and she stepped inside and headed to Reception, frowning as she approached, noticing the man that had said goodbye to his daughter standing right in front.

Was he a patient here?

She tried not to take in more details about him, because she didn't want to, but her eyes seemed to do their own thing and she couldn't help but notice how much taller he was, now that he was closer to her. How his shoes were perfectly buffed, the confidence with which he stood there as he waited for the receptionist to be free from her patient with a prescription enquiry. Then her nose betrayed her by noticing how good he smelt. Something masculine. Sandalwood? Neroli? Bergamot? She was never very good at identifying specific aftershaves or lotions that men wore.

And then the patient went to sit in the waiting room and the man in front stepped forward and she heard him say, 'Hello. I'm Dr Moore.'

Dr Moore? Dr Max Moore? Priti had told her that there were going to be three new doctors starting at the practice. A Dr Oliver Clandon, herself and a Dr Max Moore. She'd just expected, though she didn't know why, that the two men would be older. She wondered where his wife was and why she wasn't at school drop-off this morning. Maybe she started work earlier than him and it had just been more convenient for him to take their daughter in for her first day?

That had to be it, so it didn't matter that she was going to have to work with this guy that was way too handsome for his own good. He was already taken.

She stepped forward to speak to the receptionist. 'And I'm Dr Nightingale. I'm expected, too.'

Dr Moore turned to look at her, his face breaking into a friendly smile as he held out his hand for her to shake. 'Hello! It's Max.'

She took his hand and shook, but broke contact as quickly as she could without being rude. Ignoring the tingles in her hand, the shiver that ran up her arm. 'Annabella. But everyone calls me Bella.'

There was a strange pause. 'Very pleased to meet you. I guess we're going to be working together?'

She nodded. Smiled. 'I guess we are.'

Annabella. But everyone calls me Bella.

Max had been able to breathe then.

Bella. Not *Anna.* She didn't have the same name as his dead wife. And she looked nothing like her, either. His wife had been blonde, like him, Bella was dark-haired. Hair like dark chocolate. Smooth, silky. Piercing blue eyes.

He'd noticed her earlier at the school, of course. How could he not have? She'd looked so lost and alone, her son having gone to play with some other boys on the climbing frames, and Dr Nightingale—*Bella*—had stood there in the centre of the yard, arms locked around her body, gazing at her son and looking a little unwanted.

He'd felt her pain.

Max knew the feeling. Saying goodbye to Rosie this morning had been incredibly painful. His daughter had not wanted to say goodbye. She'd wanted to hold onto him. She'd been scared. She hadn't known anybody.

She'd begged him to stay with her.

His heart had ached for her. Knowing she had such a long day ahead of her. Not only a full day of school, but also an after-school club, but Miss

Celic, his daughter's teacher, had reassured him that Rosie would not be the only one to do that. There were going to be others having a long day, too, but they'd be okay, once they settled into it.

It had been hard to say goodbye. It had been hard to let her go. He'd protected her so much from the world, it felt wrong to let someone else protect her, even if they were teachers. Trained professionals. But he'd been her everything since Anna's parents had emigrated to Spain, in search of warmer climes for their health. He'd promised he'd visit them every summer holidays. Stay for a couple of weeks, so they could continue to know their granddaughter and be a part of her life. But, needing support, he'd moved here, closer to his own parents, so that they could be involved with Rosie, too. His daughter had lost a mother, much too soon. She needed as many people as possible.

Max wondered if Dr Nightingale's—Bella's— son was in the after-school club, too.

He must have asked the question out loud, because she was nodding. 'Yes, he is, but I'm not sure he's that worried about it. He couldn't wait to get into school this morning.'

'I had the opposite. I think Rosie wanted to stay with me.'

At that moment, the practice manager, Priti, arrived and welcomed them both. 'Let me introduce you to the other doctors. I think they're between patients right now.'

They met Dr Oliver Clandon first. He was an older gentleman. Distinguished. Seemed really nice and friendly. Then they were introduced to Dr Lorna Hudson. Again, older, but she had stunning red hair, wavy. Kind eyes and a bright smile. She shook their hands. 'Did you find us all right?'

'It was easy enough. Thankfully the clinic is near the infant school.'

'Oh, that's right. Priti said you'd both got young kids. How old?'

They kept their conversation short, as Lorna's computer beeped to let her know her next patient had arrived and so Priti took them to their consulting rooms. Bella first and then his room, next door to Dr Nightingale's. 'There's a welcome pack on your desk. ID card and passcode information for the computer is in the pack. You'll want to create your own password.'

'Thank you.'

'First patient is at ten o'clock. We've allocated both you and Bella twenty-minute consultations for the first day, just until you get into the swing of things and begin to learn where everything is.'

'Sounds great.'

'I'll leave you to it, but my office is just at the

end of the hall. I'm on an admin day, so, any problems, don't hesitate to knock.'

'Will do. And thank you again.'

Priti left him to it and he sat down at his desk, switched on the computer and, whilst he waited for it to boot up, he opened his backpack and removed the framed picture he'd brought with him of Anna holding Rosie in her arms, when she was just a few hours old. It was one of the few pictures he had of them together, where Anna looked well. When she still had her hair. He treasured it. Looking at it, he could almost pretend that it was just a normal picture. A mother with her newborn child. The glow and exhaustion on her face from happiness, before more horrible news hit them.

He wondered how Rosie was doing. If she'd settled. If she was okay.

He had to trust that she was, if he was going to do his job. But it felt as if a part of him were missing. Max glanced at the wall that separated him from Bella. Dr Nightingale.

She was probably feeling the exact same way.

Bella called through her first patient of the day. Her first patient ever at Clearbrook, knowing that she would remember this patient over any other, because of it.

Dorothea Godwin ambled down the corridor

towards her, leaning heavily on a walking stick and carrying a wicker bag in her other hand. 'Hello, Doctor. How are you?'

'I'm very well, thank you! Pleased to meet you. I'm Dr Nightingale.'

Behind her, the door to Max's room opened and she turned to see him waiting for his own first patient to make it down the corridor, too. Automatically, she smiled at him and his own smile was warm and comforting. Genuine. Reassuring. She felt a little bad about jumping to conclusions about him earlier, just because he was attractive. His looks didn't mean he'd be like her ex and the trust issues she'd developed since that past fiasco would need some work if she was going to make friends here. She had plans, beyond her job and Ewan's success at school, of really becoming part of the community. Of becoming social, and she knew she needed to work on herself first.

She nodded her greeting and closed the door behind her, waiting for Dorothea to settle into her chair before she took her own seat. 'It says here that you're concerned about some breathing issues you've been having?'

Every time a patient booked an appointment, the reception staff had to ask what the consultation was for, so they could make a note and add it to the clinic list. That way, the consulting physician could check the history before the appointment to see if there was anything similar in the patient's previous history, what co-morbidities there might be, but also to prepare themselves for the consult.

'That's right.'

Dorothea was breathing heavily from the short walk down the corridor from the waiting room. 'I'm just breathless a lot lately and I've never been like this before. I did have a spring cold a week ago and I wondered if it was something to do with that.'

'It's possible that a viral infection could have caused a residual lung issue, but let's have a chat first and then I'll do some obs, if that's okay with you, and see where we go from there. How does that sound?'

'Marvellous.'

'Is the breathlessness worse after movement, or is it like this all the time?'

'Both, really.'

'And you've never had any issues with asthma, or your lungs, before?'

'No. Fit as a fiddle.'

Bella performed some observations on Dorothea. Her blood pressure was a little raised, but to be expected. Her pulse was a little fast and she had a slight temperature. 'What sort of symptoms did the cold give you?'

'Well, this breathing issue. I coughed a lot. A dreadful cough for the first few days and I felt so tired.'

'Blocked nose? Headaches?'

'No, not really.'

'Okay. I'd like to do a quick swab, if that's okay? To check to see if you have Covid.' She swabbed Dorothea's nose, dipped the swab in the solution, mixed it and then added a couple of drops to the testing stick. Whilst she waited for the results, she listened to her patient's chest. She had equal sounds. No crackling. So no chest infection and her heart sounded good, no arrhythmias, or murmurs. She had no swelling in her ankles, no puffiness, no water retention. Her oxygen saturations were at ninety-three, just under what they should be at ninety-four. 'Do you live with anyone?'

'No. I enjoy my freedom too much. Believe it or not, but I used to be quite the vixen in my youth. Got plenty of offers, but never really wanted to be tied down by a man. I do have a gentleman caller, though, so I get to have some fun when I want it. On my terms!' Dorothea laughed, then coughed.

'Sounds like you have it all worked out. Good for you.'

Dorothea chuckled. 'Indeed. I saw what my own mother went through and knew I didn't want that for myself. It was odd for women, back in my day, to not want marriage, but I made it work and all those people who thought I was odd are a little bit jealous now.'

Bella nodded. She could remember her own mum telling her that little girls grew up to get married and have children of their own and it would bring her happiness, but all her own personal heartbreak had come from romantic relationships. 'You have Covid.'

'No! But I'm vaccinated!'

'The vaccination doesn't stop you from getting Covid. It just stops it from getting really bad and putting you in hospital.'

'So the breathlessness is down to that little bugger, then, is it?'

'I'm afraid so. You might just need to take it easy for a little while. But I can prescribe you an inhaler to use that should help things, if you feel like you'd need it.'

Dorothea nodded. 'Better to have something and not need it than need something and not have it.'

'My thoughts exactly.' Bella made up the prescription. 'I've sent that order through to your named chemist. You should be able to pick it up this afternoon.' She paused. 'Maybe get your gentleman caller to look after you a little bit.'

'Ernest would love to move in and nurse me, I'll give you that, but what about my social life?'

'How do you mean?'

'I go to a lot of clubs and groups. I have an art class every Monday evening. I have that tonight. So far, it's been fruit in bowls and still life and all that.' Dorothea leaned in. 'But tonight, we've got a life model. A male life model!'

Bella laughed. 'Good thing I've prescribed you that inhaler, then!'

'Can I go to the class with this Covid thing?'

'People aren't that upset about it these days. It would be best for you to stay in, to help prevent spread, but no one's going to stop you. You could always wear a mask and warn everyone.'

'Ooh, good! I'll do that, then! Let the male model think I'm breathless from Covid. You've been very nice.' Dorothea's gaze dropped to her hand. 'I don't see a ring. Are you not married either?'

Bella didn't like to discuss her own life with her patients. Not if she could help it. 'No, but I do have a little boy who is the love of my life and that's all I need.'

Dorothea stood. 'Motherly love is a wonderful thing, but—' she winked '—no substitute for a warm body in bed with you! That wonderful little boy will grow into a man and will *leave you* for someone else. If you don't want to be alone, you have to get out there.'

Bella laughed awkwardly and said goodbye to Dorothea and watched her walk down the corridor back out to Reception and then she went back into her consulting room and closed the door.

She'd never minded being alone. Had sworn off the idea of marriage. Had sworn off the idea of men completely. But Dorothea was right. It had been a long time since a man had lain in a bed with her. Since she had allowed a man to be with her. Since she'd had someone to be vulnerable with.

She thought of Max's smiling face, lying on a pillow next to hers, and instantly she stopped typing.

I can't think of him like that! He's married.

Probably. And even if he wasn't, he'd no doubt have a long line of women who would be more than happy to jump into bed with him and he would not consider an insecure single mother with trust issues.

That wasn't sexy.

Bella had Ewan and, yes, one day he would move out. One day he *would* start a life of his own, but he would always *come back* and visit his mum, because they were close and had a strong bond and that would never change.

And it would be enough.

It would always be enough.

She reached for her bag and found the paracetamol. Her headache was bad today and so she took two, hoping they would help.

They usually did.

CHAPTER TWO

MAX'S FIRST PATIENT, a Mr Robert Heaney, came down the corridor, limping. The consult note said 'pain in left leg' and it was vague enough to be any number of possible reasons. So he invited Mr Heaney in and settled down into his seat. 'How can I help you today?'

'It's my leg. This one.' Mr Heaney patted his left knee. 'Been causing me a problem for about a week now with this pain in my calf.'

Max nodded. 'Is it something that's come on suddenly?'

'I guess. One day it was fine and I could get about no problem, the next day, it's hurting me.'

'And have you banged the leg? Had a fall? Injured it in any way?'

'No, nothing like that. I am an active man, so I've noticed it a lot. I do a lot of walking and a lot of gardening and when it first started, I just imagined I'd maybe pulled it or something and imagined it would go away, but it hasn't.'

'And would you say the leg looks different? Is it swollen, or red, or hot?'

'A bit.'

'And what is the pain like? Is it a sharp, stabbing pain, or more like an ache?'

'It throbs. Like in pulses.'

'All right, well, maybe we ought to take a look at it. Can you raise your trouser leg above it, or would it be better for you to remove them?'

'I'll have to take them off.' Mr Heaney stood and began to drop his trousers, before Max could offer him a chaperone.

His patient's left calf muscle did look more swollen than the right and there was a redness and a heat to it. Max took a tape measure and measured the circumference of both calf muscles and the left one was a couple of inches larger than the right. 'Well, this could be a simple infection, but the thing we're worried about the most with symptoms like this is a DVT. A deep vein thrombosis.' A blood clot. It could be worrying in case the clot spread to the lungs and caused a pulmonary embolism. It could be life-threatening. 'Any chest pains? Any breathlessness?'

'No.' Mr Heaney shook his head. 'Is this because I went on holiday to Barcelona?'

'When was that?'

'Just over a week ago. Went on a stag do. My future son-in-law's.'

'If it is a blood clot, then that is possible. What I'd like to do is refer you to hospital immediately for an ultrasound scan. Would you be able to get there? Is there someone who could drive you?'

'My wife.'

'Good. I'll print out this letter for you to take with you and you'll be seen as quickly as they can. I'll call through to them now.' Max found the details for the local hospital and followed the protocols for a DVT referral.

'And if it is?' Mr Heaney asked when Max got off the phone. 'Is that surgery?'

'It can be. They'll also prescribe blood thinners for you to take afterwards. Maybe warfarin or rivaroxaban.'

'Never thought I'd get something like this.' He seemed shocked.

'It can happen to anyone. Any time and sometimes for no reason at all that we can determine.' He passed his patient the letter. 'Good luck. I hope they're able to sort it out for you quickly.'

'Thank you, Doctor.'

'Bye.'

That was the thing with many health conditions. You could feel perfectly fine, completely unaware of something malignant growing inside. He remembered a great aunt of his own, who had lived to the grand old age of ninety-four. She'd seemed fine. Healthy as a horse. Had never been sick a day in her life. Then one day, right after lunch, she'd passed out. Hit her head on the way down and was taken to hospital and there, during a scan, they'd discovered that her body was riddled with tumours and she'd passed away two weeks later.

But she'd had no pain. No discomfort to tell her that something was wrong. She'd still been attending all her groups. Still laughing. Still enjoying her nightly tipple of whisky before bed—her only vice. In those last two weeks, the whisky had been exchanged for morphine.

And then there was his own wife, Anna. She'd been the picture of health. Glowing. Happy. She'd fallen pregnant—accidentally, but they'd adapted to the news. And then, at four months, she'd discovered a lump. Thought it nothing more than a cyst.

But it hadn't been.

You never know what life might suddenly throw at you. What curveballs you'll have to deal with.

Max picked up the framed picture of his wife and baby daughter. How much he wished they could have had more time. But it had been short. Fleeting. And now he was alone with Rosie, try-ing to be the best father he could be.

He had four more patients to see before morning break. He met a very nice young lady who wanted to discuss going on the contraceptive pill. A young boy of four with chicken pox. An elderly gent with back pain, having spent too long in the garden over the weekend, and his last patient before break was a young woman who came in looking pale and red-eyed, pushing a pram with her three-week-old baby son in.

'I feel nothing,' she said, before she burst into tears and he had to pass her the box of tissues that had been sitting on the window ledge.

Max waited for her tears to dry up and encouraged her to speak more.

'Since having baby Hayden, I just… I don't feel any joy. I don't feel anything…for him.' She indicated the baby and began to cry some more. 'I should, right? I should feel something! I should be totally in love with him and yet all I feel is numbness and sometimes resentment that my life has changed and what for? My life is harder now. I'm not sleeping. I'm not eating. Hayden cries all the time. I'm left alone all day with the baby, because my husband works and I can't tell *him* how I feel.'

At that moment, Hayden seemed to wake and began to fuss and so Max got up and scooped the baby out of his pram and gently began to sway with him and pat his back in case he had trapped wind, and waited for his mother, Rachel, to stop crying.

'What you're feeling is totally normal. Bonds don't always immediately appear because you want them to, or because the media or online influencers paint a picture of domestic and maternal bliss with their babies. Your body has been through an enormous change. You're flooded with hormones and you're adapting to a new dynamic, whilst trying to take care of a brand-new baby human. It's okay to feel this way, to feel a little blue after birth. We call it postnatal depression and it's normal, but it doesn't mean it'll last and it doesn't mean you will always feel this way. Now, let me assess little Hayden to see if there's a reason for the crying.'

Baby Hayden was fine. He'd put on a few ounces since his birth weight, his reflexes were good, his chest and tummy sounded fine and Rachel said he was having wet nappies and breast-feeding well.

'He could just be a little colicky, which is common.' Colic was when a baby cried a lot for no apparent reason. It made them hard to soothe, they'd clench their fists, go red in the face and bring their knees up, indicating perhaps a little discomfort in their stomach. 'It does pass, usually around three to four months. You can get anti-colic drops and you can make sure you're not eating spicy foods or anything that might upset him, but honestly? I can't promise you that these things will work. What you need to do more than anything else is to give yourself a lot more grace. Make sure you rest. Nap when Hayden sleeps. Eat well. Drink plenty. Try and get outside each day if you can—the exercise and fresh air will do you both good.'

Max remembered the first few weeks after Rosie's birth, when the bad news of Anna's condition had got worse and instead of being allowed to enjoy those first few weeks with her baby, she'd got to sit in hospitals, enduring chemotherapy.

He'd taken Rosie on those outdoor walks alone. They'd spent many hours in the parks, or walking the trails, and he'd talk to his daughter as they went, telling her all about the ducks and the trees and the flowers, but most of all, about the beautiful and wondrous person that was Rosie's mother. How he hoped that Rosie would be able to form memories with her mother that she would be able to remember for herself. A hope that she was never able to accomplish.

Rosie had no memory of her mother. She'd been too young when Anna had passed and he'd had to raise his daughter alone. Fiercely loving her and protecting her and making sure she wanted for nothing, but fearing all the time that he wasn't enough for her. That her lack of a mother in her life would somehow hold her back. Make her less confident. As she had been that morning about going into school.

'Are you able to sit down with your husband and tell him how you're feeling? I think you'll be surprised that he probably feels just as over-whelmed as you do.'

'But I'm meant to know what to do as a mother. How to soothe my baby and I can't sometimes. It's like he hates me.'

'And it bothers you. You care about it. Which shows that you *do* have feelings. You are at-tached. You do love your baby, it just takes time, sometimes, before that bond blooms and you'll reach a point where you can't remember not lov-ing him.'

'I hope so.'

'Is there the possibility that your husband can give you some alone time? So you get a break? Time to shower? To meet with friends?'

'We haven't spoken about it.'

'Perhaps you should try. I'm sure he'd under-stand. Have you spoken to your health visitor about this?'

Rachel shook her head.

'Well, I'll inform her for you. Get her to check in on you a little more often, but I'd also like to see you, maybe in another week? See how you are? And if you feel like it's getting worse, or you're not coping at all, you ring the surgery and I'll see you, all right? I'll leave word with Reception that if you call, they're to fit you in somehow. I'll make time for you.'

'Thank you.' She burst into tears again. As if that one small act of kindness was all too much.

He bid her farewell, wishing that there'd been some sort of magic button he could press to make her world all right again. *He* knew she would get over this. He knew there was light on the other side for Rachel. But she couldn't see it yet, because she was still in the trenches, feeling guilty that she wasn't being the mother she imagined she was meant to be.

He felt her pain.

Max made his way to the staffroom. He was the only person there and so he rummaged in the cupboards and found a box of peppermint teabags and switched on the kettle. As he waited for it to boil, he picked up a magazine off the low coffee table and began to read, putting it down again when Dr Nightingale—Bella—entered.

'Hey. How's it going?' he asked.

'Good, I think. You?'

'Same.'

'Feels good to finally be putting down some personal roots and not living the locum life any more.'

'I know exactly what you mean. I felt like a jobbing doctor, picking up the occasional shift here and there, but never staying in one place long enough to make any real friends at work. Fancy a tea? I've got the kettle on.'

'Do they have anything herbal?'

'There's peppermint. That's what I'm having and I think I saw a lemon and ginger one in there, too.'

'Peppermint will be great, thanks.' She sat down beside him, looking quite nervous and apprehensive, tucking her long, dark hair behind one ear.

She had beautiful skin, he noticed. Like porcelain. If she'd been an actress, she'd have made an excellent vampire. He smiled.

'What?' She caught him smiling.

'Nothing. Peppermint, you say?' he said, trying to distract as he got up to make her drink, too.

'Yes. Please. No sign of Lorna or Oliver?'

'I think I heard him take a drink down to her room.'

'Oh. Do they know each other, then?'

'Erm, I think I remember Priti saying something along the lines of them knowing each other at medical school.'

'Wow. They must have a lot to catch up on, then.'

'Yep.'

'Must be strange for the two of them to meet up again after all those years.'

It had to be. But kind of nice, too, he thought. 'How do you think our kids are getting on?'

Bella laughed. 'Ewan's probably taken over the whole school by now. I'd hoped for a wistful cuddle before he went in, but he couldn't wait to get in there. Don't think he's even thought about me. He couldn't wait to be off.'

'But that's good, right? That you've imbued him with such confidence? I wish Rosie had a little of that. Might put my mind at rest, knowing she's got such a long day ahead of her without me.'

'Have you ever been apart?'

'She's spent some time with her grandparents. The occasional sleepover, you know, but that's with people that she's grown up with. That she knows. Miss Celic, the school, all those other kids, they're all strange.'

'She'll be okay. Even if she doesn't think so right now, she will be.'

'It's hard though. Being a single parent. Trying to be both a mother and a father to your child. Rosie's mum, she…er…she died. When Rosie was one year old.'

'I'm so sorry to hear that.' She looked surprised too. Her sympathy sincere. 'What happened? If you don't mind me asking?'

'Anna discovered she had breast cancer at the beginning of her pregnancy. It was aggressive and we were actually advised to terminate, so that she could receive treatment.'

'Oh. That must have been awful for you both.'

The way she was looking at him was intense. He was taken in by the inviting blue of her eyes. The way she seemed to understand the pain they'd been in at being told such a thing. 'It was. I told Anna I'd support her either way, but that I agreed with the doctors. Anna though? She didn't. She wanted to be a mother and she felt so well she didn't want to terminate, convinced she could beat the cancer. She was induced early. Thirty-six weeks, but tests afterwards showed that the cancer had metastasised and that all they could offer her was palliative chemotherapy.'

'My God...' Bella looked down at the floor. 'I'm so sorry.'

'It's been me and Rosie ever since. It's been hard, but I think we're doing okay. Anna's parents emigrated recently, due to their own health, seeking warmer climes, and so, knowing I wanted to give Rosie some stability, I moved here to be closer to my parents, so that she had family that wasn't just me.'

He paused, thinking about all the stress he'd

gone through when he'd heard that Morag and Jim, Anna's parents, were leaving. They'd been his rock. His connection to Anna and now even they were gone.

'What about you? Are you here with Ewan's dad?'

Bella smiled and shook her head sadly. 'No, I'm not. I'm a single parent like you.'

He nodded. 'I see. Does Ewan get to see his dad?'

'No.' Bella sucked in a deep breath and looked everywhere but at him.

Had he overstepped?

'Blake was cheating on me. I found that out the day I discovered I was pregnant with Ewan. I moved out—we'd been living together, and I left the door open for him to be a part of Ewan's life, but he didn't want to know. He pays child support, but that's all we get from him. Not a card, not a present. He didn't even come to see his son when he was born. But, you know, we've accepted that and moved on and I think I'm doing a half-decent job at raising a little boy that will grow up to respect women and not cheat on them. And...' she laughed '...he's clearly confident.'

Max smiled. 'Well, from what I saw today, you've raised a very happy little boy.'

'Thank you.'

He passed her a mug of peppermint tea. 'And what do you do when you're not raising a man of the future?'

'Sleep!' She laughed, accepting it. 'I like to read. Fiction. I also dabble with drawing and painting, but I'm not very good.'

'Seriously? I like doing that, too. You should show me your work.'

'Oh, I don't think it's anything that should be endured by the public.'

'You show me yours. I'll show you mine.' He winked at her and laughed when she blushed and looked away.

He loved the way she blushed. That creamy porcelain skin gently glowed with a hint of pink. A small bloom of warmth on each cheek that slowly dissipated again back to the vampire white.

'I guess we'd better get back to it?'

She nodded. 'Yes.'

'I'll see you later.'

She raised her mug. 'Yes. And thank you. For my peppermint tea.'

'You're welcome, Bella. You're very welcome.'

Even though she'd enjoyed her first day, her heart ached for Ewan. She had missed him so much. And once her admin for the day and her telephone appointments had been completed, she grabbed her things from the staffroom and hurried to the infants' school to collect from the after-school club.

She imagined she'd find a very tired young boy. She imagined that when she walked through the door to collect him, he would see her and run into her arms for a kiss and a big hug. And then he would babble excitedly about all the things he'd done that day as they walked home and maybe she'd have some art to pin up on the fridge.

But when she arrived at the school, the kids were all outside playing in the playground on the climbing equipment and she could see Ewan at the top of the climbing frame, laughing with his new friends and, though she hated to call him down, she knew she had to get his attention. 'Ewan! Ewan, I'm here now. We can go home!'

One of the staff came over to her. 'You're Ewan's mum?'

'Yes, that's right. How's he been?'

'Brilliant. That's a happy boy you've got there. Very confident. Wasn't shy about joining in or leading the group.'

Bella was glad to hear it. 'Has he eaten?'

'Just some fruit slices. He was more interested in playing pirates with the other boys over there.'

She nodded, watching as Ewan reluctantly began his climb down. She couldn't see Rosie and she had to be here, because when Bella had left work, Max had still been working on some prescription requests.

'I'll take you in, so you can pick up his coat and bag,' said the staff member.

'Oh, right. Of course.' Reluctantly, she headed inside, feeling as though she'd have to postpone that hug and kiss for a little while longer.

Inside, there was a small kitchenette, where another member of staff was washing some multicoloured plastic plates and forks and spoons. She wore a tabard with teddy bears on it. 'This is Ewan's mum.'

The tabard lady nodded and smiled.

Past the kitchenette was a room filled with lumpy sofas, beanbags and boxes of toys and puzzles, a TV in a corner, with a games console and a messy bookshelf. Next to the bookshelf was Rosie. Curled up on a chair with a member of staff, having a story read to her. The little girl looked so tired. So overwhelmed, her cheeks red, her eyes puffy, as if she'd been crying for a long time, that even Bella felt her heart ache for her.

Once she'd collected Ewan's coat and bag, she took a moment to go over to her. 'It's Rosie, isn't it?' Bella knelt down, to be on the little girl's level.

Rosie nodded, uncertainly.

'My name's Bella and I work with your dad. He'll be here soon. You won't have to wait too much longer.'

'Really?' Rosie looked hopeful, the hint of a smile breaking across her face as she glanced at the doorway, as if expecting her dad to walk through any moment.

Bella smiled back. 'Really. I'm Ewan's mummy. My name's Bella. I'm a doctor, like your dad.'

At that moment, the door swung open and in walked Ewan. 'Mummy!'

She stood and held out her arms as he ran straight into them for a hug, a hug that she hoped would last for minutes, if not hours, as she so needed to feel his body pressed against hers. But the second he held her, the second he let go to reel off an impressive list of all the things that he'd got up to that day. 'Slow down, slow down! Wow. Okay. First things first. Coat on.'

He slid his arms into his coat and she passed him his bag. 'Ewan, have you met Rosie?'

Ewan glanced at the little girl. 'No.'

'I need you to be friends with her, okay? Look after her.'

He nodded. 'Okay.' And then he did some-thing that was very sweet. He walked over to her and held out his hand. Just as she'd taught him to. 'Hello, Rosie. My name's Ewan. Do you want to be my friend?'

Very shyly, Rosie nodded and shook his hand.

Then Ewan turned to her. 'Can we go home now? I'm *starving*!'

She chuckled. 'Yes. Me too, but…' She turned back to Rosie. 'Do you want us to wait with you until your dad gets here?'

Rosie shook her head. 'I'm okay.'

'All right. Well, we'll see you tomorrow?'

Rosie nodded.

When Max arrived at the school, he found his daughter snuggled into a member of staff on the couch, being read a story. Her cheeks were flushed and she looked so very tired and instantly he felt guilty for subjecting her to such a long day.

Maybe it was too soon?

Maybe going back to work like this, accepting a full-time job like this, wasn't fair on her? But the second she saw him, her face brightened and she ran across the floor to him and threw herself into his arms as he scooped her up and swung her around, before pulling her in for a long, long hug. 'Oh, I've missed you! Are you okay?'

The staff member who'd been reading her the story got up and smiled at him. 'She's been fine. A little teary to start with, but that's to be expected. We've just been enjoying this story. Do you want to take it home with you? Finish it at bedtime?'

It felt good to hold Rosie in his arms. Her little, lightweight body. He'd missed her so much. Had worried about her all day. Had she thought he'd abandoned her? Despite all the talks they'd had about what this day would look like? Feel like? 'Thank you.' He took the book and kissed his daughter's cheek. 'Ready to go home?' he whispered.

He felt her nod and so, without putting her down, he grabbed her coat and the teacher put the book into her bag and passed him that and she mouthed goodbye and he left, feeling his heart lighten the further and further away they got.

He would get her home, feed her, bathe her, put her to bed.

And do it all again tomorrow.

Would it get easier?

Max stroked her back as he walked with her in his arms. He didn't care what anyone might think, he would carry his daughter for as long as she would let him, because one day she'd be too old for it and he never wanted to think about that. Or those difficult teenager years when perhaps she might be embarrassed by him and ask him to walk about ten yards behind her to pretend they weren't together.

When they got back to their new home, a cottage on Field Lane, he finally put her down to search for his keys and open the door.

Rosie ran inside and headed for the kitchen.

'Hungry?'

She nodded.

He opened the fridge. 'We've got…pizza? How does that sound?'

She beamed. 'Pizza! Pepperoni?'

'Is there any other kind?' He grabbed the pizza and placed it in the oven and, whilst it was cooking, he got some salad bits out and began to prepare a side. 'So, how was your first day?'

'Okay.'

'You make any friends?'

'A boy.'

'A boy?' He turned around, surprised. He'd always viewed Rosie as a girl's girl. He'd never imagined her making friends with a boy first. 'What's his name?'

'Ewan.'

Max smiled. Bella's son. 'Okay. Is he nice?'

Rosie nodded. 'Mmm-hmm. Can I help you cut things up?'

He had some child-friendly knives, so he let her slice the cucumber.

'Bella's nice, too.'

He stopped to look at her. 'You met Bella?'

'She said hello to me. She's a doctor, too. Like you.'

'That's right. You liked her?'

Another nod. 'Did she offer to be your friend, too?'

Max smiled. 'Yes. Yes, she did. I think we're going to be very good friends.'

'So you had a good first day, too?'

He kissed the top of her head. She was saying she had a good first day. It helped leach away some of the guilt he'd been feeling. 'Yeah. A great first day.'

CHAPTER THREE

BELLA HAD SLEPT much better last night than she had the night before, but still she woke with one of her usual headaches she'd been having lately. Sighing, she popped a couple of pain-killers whilst Ewan ate his breakfast and then checked his bag to make sure he had everything he needed for the day.

'Where are your plimsolls?'

'I don't know.'

'They were in here yesterday. How could they have disappeared?'

'I don't know.' He wasn't really listening. He was watching cartoons whilst spooning cereal into his mouth.

Bella sighed. She'd have to ask at the school, or check the lost-property box, but it was an-noying, because they were brand new. 'Ten min-utes!' she called, as post dropped through the letter box and she headed down the hallway to collect it.

Two letters confirming that she was now a

new customer of a couple of utility companies and one letter that looked as if it was from the hospital. Before they'd moved here, she'd been to see her own doctor about the headaches she'd been having. She was sure they were just migraines, but, better to be safe than sorry, her GP had referred her to a neurologist. The neurologist in question worked at three different hospitals and one of them happened to be at the hospital closest to Clearbrook.

Opening the envelope, she discovered that she had an appointment in a few weeks' time. She made a note of the date and time in her phone, so that she could inform Priti that she wouldn't be in that afternoon and to rearrange her clinic for that day. It said on the letter to allow three hours for the appointment, in case she had to have a scan, so unfortunately it would mean missing half a day.

'Come on, we don't want to be late. Go brush your teeth.' Ewan scampered upstairs and Bella turned off the television and checked her own bag and reflection in the mirror. Pale, as always, though the bags under her eyes looked the same. She dabbed some concealer on them and hoped for the best. No one wanted to visit a doctor who looked ill themselves. It hardly inspired confidence.

The concealer helped and she told herself that

all she needed were a few more decent nights' sleep. It was stressful—moving home to a new area where you knew no one. Starting a new job. A full-time job. Sending your kid to school for the first time. They'd both been through some big changes. She was trying to separate herself from the past. Their last home had been nice, but it had been the place where everything had gone wrong and it felt tainted somehow.

Starting anew, turning over a new page, felt like the start they both needed. The doctors at Clearbrook were great and Max was... She flushed, pushing the image of his face on her pillow away. Max was a nice guy, but she had zero intentions of getting involved with him. What she needed to do was find a way to integrate into the rest of Clearbrook society. Maybe there was a book club or supper club she could join.

That might be good. Maybe an art class? I ought to have asked Dorothea for the details...

Ewan came running back downstairs, full of beans and ready for a new day.

'You get the teeth at the back?'

'Yes, Mummy.'

'You brushed for two minutes?'

'Yes.'

'You set the timer?'

'Yes!'

She smiled at him and ruffled his dark hair,

before helping him on with his coat. Then she grabbed her own bag and jacket and headed on out.

They were walking down their front path, when Bella spotted movement at the cottage opposite and slowed down, unable to believe her eyes.

Max? And Rosie?

He'd spotted her, too, and had the same look on his face that she must have had on her own. Surprise. Shock. But pleasant surprise, at least.

She'd just been thinking about him. Embarrassed, she hoped she wasn't flushed in the face.

'Hello, you two. What are you doing here?' Max asked.

'We live here.'

'So do we.'

'What, here? On Field Lane?' She couldn't quite believe it.

'We're renting from Dr Mossman, who used to work at the practice.'

'So am I!' She remembered the kindly old gentleman telling her as she signed the rental agreement that he had a few cottages that he owned in the village. That he'd bought them when he was in his fifties, to help fund his retirement. That his wife had enjoyed doing up the properties, because she used to be an interior designer and so it had become a project for them both.

Rosie was clinging to her dad's leg, but she peered from behind him and gave Bella a shy smile.

'Morning, Rosie.'

'Hi,' she answered, shyly.

'Are you on your way to school?' Max asked.

'Yes.'

'We might as well walk together, then, if that's okay?'

She couldn't think of a way to say no without being rude, but it unnerved her. Working with Max was one thing. There was a distance that was created, a line that was drawn, when someone was your colleague. But being with them away from work? In your free time? And doing so willingly? That made him more than a colleague, somehow, and his dashing good looks and easy charm made her uneasy. She was already drawn to his friendly warmth. His smile. His twinkling eyes. And she didn't want to be. Before, she'd allowed a man's dashing good looks to blind her to the small red flags and she didn't want to make that mistake again.

Her ex, Blake, had been handsome and effortlessly charming. He'd been that way with every woman, but he'd made her feel as if she were his whole world and she'd been the one he'd come home to at night. But he'd been the ultimate snake and the worst of it was—she'd been totally blindsided by him. He'd told her she was beautiful, whispered sweet nothings into her ears most nights, but it had all been part of his ruse. To make her feel as though she didn't have to worry about him. That she didn't have to doubt the strength of his love.

And so when he'd started going to the gym three times a week, she'd been happy that he'd found something else he'd loved. But he hadn't just been working out with weights, but with another woman. He'd come back buffed, but that was because his physical workouts had been sexually athletic, as well as on the elliptical. And he'd always come back so pleased with himself, telling her about his gains and what he'd managed to lift, and she'd been so happy for him. Even encouraged him to go more, seeing as he'd been enjoying it so much.

I was such a fool.

Bella had felt humiliated when she'd discovered the truth of his deception. Belittled. Naïve. And she'd sworn to herself never to be taken in by a handsome man with a stunning countenance ever again.

Glancing sideways, she stole a glance at Max as if to see if she could see anything about him that might give away secrets and lies, but there was nothing there. He seemed genuine, but she couldn't possibly risk it.

Ewan and Rosie walked together, ahead of them. She could hear him babbling away to Rosie about the biggest worm he'd ever found and she couldn't help but smile at him.

'Rosie told me you met yesterday,' Max said.

'Oh, yes. At the after-school club. She looked so tired, bless her, and I just wanted her to know that you were right behind me and she wouldn't have to wait much longer. I offered to wait with her.'

'She told me. She liked you. That you were very nice to her.'

Bella smiled. 'I told Ewan to be her friend. I hope that's okay?'

'Of course, it is!'

'I still can't quite believe that we're neighbours.'

He laughed. 'No. Nor me. But I guess we should have figured it out. Trying to buy a place in Clearbrook is incredibly difficult. The fact that we've both managed to rent somewhere should have been a clue. Dr Mossman told he owns almost the whole street in Field Lane.'

'He's probably got a nice comfy retirement ahead of him, then.'

'Probably. You know what would be nice? And we only have to do it if you're okay with it, but we'll both be walking to school each morning before work—we could arrange to meet up each time and walk in together. That way the kids can get to know one another more.'

It seemed such a simple, nice and easy suggestion. And he meant it as friends and neighbours, surely nothing more than that? But could it be a ruse for something else? They would spend all day with each other at work anyway…

Relax, Bella. Remember those trust issues you promised yourself you'd work on?

'Erm…okay.'

Max glanced at his watch. 'Eight-fifteen each day?'

'Sure.' She nodded and smiled, her heart fluttering in her chest at the idea of meeting up with him every day to walk into school and then—*oh, my goodness, on our own*—walking into work! 'We'd better tell people at work we're neighbours. Don't want them thinking the wrong thing!' She could just imagine the awful gossip that might start if they didn't make it clear to everyone.

'I'm sure they wouldn't think anything untoward. Lorna and Oliver are good friends and that's understandable—they know one another from way back—and you and I are good friends because we're living opposite one another, we work together and we're both pretty much the same age and single parents. It just makes sense.'

When he put it like that, of course it made

sense. But Blake used to make things sound like good sense, too. Make things sound reasonable when all along he was a cheating, lying scumbag, seeing another woman behind her back. The people at work could still jump to conclusions about them. People naturally tried to matchmake. They couldn't help it.

But I should give him the chance to be my friend, right?

Wasn't that why she was here in Clearbrook? To make a fresh start? To make friends and connections? Max could become a very valuable friend, if she just allowed herself to give him the chance and ignored how handsome he was. How drawn she was to stare into his eyes.

As they reached the school, they stood by the gates and watched as Ewan introduced Rosie to some of the friends he'd made the day before and Rosie got invited to play on the climbing frame with the others. She glanced back at her dad, as if asking for permission. He gave her a thumbs up and she smiled and hurried after Ewan.

'She's going to get braver every day,' Max said, watching his daughter with pride in his smile. 'Makes me feel better about leaving her today. Yesterday was so hard, knowing she didn't want to go in, but she told me later that their teacher is nice.'

'Ewan said the same thing about Miss Celic.'

They stood together watching the kids play for a while, then the bell rang and the teachers came out to gather the children to their individual classes. Rosie came back to give her dad a hug and walked over to join the line. Ewan didn't come back for a hug. He just lined up behind Rosie and turned to give his mum a wave.

'How easily they let you go,' she said.

'It's because you did such a great job raising him.' Max touched her arm, probably without thinking. Probably casually, without any intent for its meaning. Just a *Hey, I see you, fellow single parent. You've done a great job.*

But Bella felt a frisson of something tremble through her. An awakening. An awareness. Of course, she found Max attractive. Maybe that was the problem! And no man had touched her for years. And it wasn't as if she were bereft of contact. Ewan hugged her all the time. He climbed into bed with her in the mornings, sometimes, but that was different. Innocent. Her son. Her little boy showing his mummy some love and she loved their snuggles that they had.

But it didn't stop her from feeling lonely. It didn't stop her from craving the touch of a lover. That was a different kind of touch. A touch that told her she mattered in a different kind of way. That she was important to someone else. A touch that was just for her and nobody else.

Having Max touch her, however innocently, reminded her of the ache that she felt at losing the father of her child. At losing a relationship that she'd thought would end with her walking down an aisle in a white dress. His touch reminded her of all that she had lost and yearned for, yet was scared to have.

When the kids disappeared inside, they turned and began to walk to work. It was only a few minutes' walk, but she felt as if it would feel like aeons.

'So, tell me more about your art,' Max asked her.

Bella laughed. 'You make me sound like a professional painter.'

Max laughed. 'Aren't you?'

'Do zentangles count?' She smiled, thinking of the type of art she did like to indulge in.

Zentangles were a collection of structured patterns. Those patterns were called tangles and you could create combinations of tangles such as lines, cross-hatching, dots, curves and shapes. No great skill was required, which was why she liked it.

'Absolutely! Are they like mandalas?'

'Kind of.' She pulled out her phone and did an Internet image search for zentangles and showed him the screen.

'Cool.'

'I find it relaxing, especially if I'm feeling a little stressed.'

'You feel stressed often?'

She laughed. 'You sound like a doctor.'

He laughed, too. 'That's good. I'm glad that I do. Do you think we get stressed because we're single parents and we have no one to share the burden with?'

'Possibly.'

'I read to get rid of stress. Reading is huge for me. I've always got a book on the go. Try to read a chapter or two before bed each night. And you're not going to believe this, but I once fancied myself a bit of an artist. You should come over one night and look at my etchings.' He laughed out loud and she blushed, madly, but laughed, too. 'Seriously, I have one or two of my drawings up on the walls in the hallway.'

'Seriously?'

'Yep.'

'What are they?'

'Wild animals, mostly. I used art as a way to escape the reality of what Rosie's mum was going through. There were many long hours spent in oncology wards and treatment rooms.'

'It must have been incredibly hard for you both.'

He shrugged. 'It was harder for Anna. When you get pregnant and have a baby, everyone expects you to be happy. To be in celebratory mood. Or sleep-deprived. Our families wanted to celebrate Rosie's arrival, but felt like they couldn't fully, because of what Anna was going through.'

'How did your wife deal with it? The new baby and fighting cancer?'

He smiled. 'She was strong. Stronger than me, that's for sure. Never complained. Not once. She said that she felt that she couldn't, because she'd made the choice to continue with the pregnancy, rather than start treatment early, and so it was all on her and she would take the consequences.' He sighed. 'I used to tell her that she was allowed to be angry. That if she needed to shout and scream, then she could, but she never did. She just wanted to hold Rosie as much as she could and love her as much as she could. Until she couldn't.'

Bella turned to look at the man beside her. The widower. The single father. A doctor. Her colleague. Neighbour. *Friend.* She couldn't imagine going through such pain. Couldn't imagine having to make a choice between continuing with a pregnancy, or aborting it to fight for her own life. To hope for a future pregnancy much further down the line. What kind of strength had it taken, in the face of all those doctors advising her to terminate, to say, *'No. I'm keeping it.'*?

She cast her mind back to the day she'd discovered she was pregnant with Ewan. Discovered that Blake had been cheating on her and that he didn't want to be a father. A friend had asked her, in the days after the break-up, when she'd still been reeling from having moved out, if she was going to keep the baby. There'd been absolutely no doubt in her mind that she was going to continue with the pregnancy. The baby had not cheated on her. It wasn't the baby's fault and, though she'd worried about the future, though she'd worried that every time she'd look at her child, she'd see Blake, it had not been enough to deter her. The second that line had turned pink, she had felt protective of the tiny bean growing deep in her womb and her protective instincts had appeared as if from nowhere.

Maybe Anna had felt the same? Bella couldn't imagine being placed in Anna's situation. What would she have done?

I'd have done the same.

She felt a strange connection to Anna, then. A unity. An understanding. And she knew without a doubt that Anna Moore, Max's wife, must have been one hell of a brave woman.

When they arrived at work, they said hello to everyone. Lorna had brought in some lemon drizzle cake that she'd baked for everyone and it sat neatly by the kettle, in a cake tin, ready for everyone to enjoy at morning break.

'Let's see what today brings!' said Max.

She'd nodded and smiled at him. How quickly a single day could change things. Yesterday, she'd been worried about him being so attractive. Had worried about her attraction to him. Had told herself she would keep him at arm's length, because of it. And yet today, in the matter of an hour, she'd discovered that they were neighbours and she'd learned more of his past, connected with his wife and suddenly he didn't seem such a threat to her any more.

She'd thought, because of his looks, that he must have led a charmed life. That it was easy for him and good things happened to him and that he probably took what he wanted and life just gave it to him.

But he was just as tortured and damaged as everyone else and she felt bad for judging him.

Turns out you never can tell what someone is going through.

He wasn't narcissistic. He wasn't Blake.

He was like her. Just trying to get through each day.

And Bella resolved, there and then, not to be so standoffish and to enjoy being his friend. On her way to her own room, she knocked on Priti's door and went in to tell her about needing the afternoon off in a few weeks' time.

He'd not mentioned to Bella that when he'd told her that he'd encouraged Anna to be angry about her prognosis, he himself had been angry.

Anger was not an attractive quality, especially in a man, and a lot of people could be scared about it, but he remembered being immensely angry at discovering his wife's cancer had spread during the months of her pregnancy and had become terminal.

He'd been angry at himself, for not persuading Anna more to terminate the pregnancy. He'd been angry at the world for threatening to take his wife from him. And yes, he'd been angry at the idea that he would eventually be left alone to raise a child whose life had caused Anna to lose her own.

Max had not wanted to resent Rosie. Of course not. It wasn't her fault. She'd not made the choice to stay and it had taken both he and Anna to make a baby, no matter how accidentally. And Anna had only examined her breasts so early in the pregnancy because a midwife had mentioned it.

As Rosie had thrived, getting bigger and glowing with health, his wife had got sicker, thinner, paler. Weaker. As Rosie had begun to develop, learning how to sit, crawl, walk, Anna had begun to be more bedbound. It had almost been as if the umbilical cord had still been there and that somehow Rosie were taking all of Anna's vitality.

It had been a difficult year and then, days after Rosie had turned one and they'd celebrated her birthday in Anna's hospice room, surrounded by balloons still, his wife had finally passed away. Quietly. Without fanfare. In her sleep.

Three had become two.

He'd not known how to be. How to get through the days. Anna's parents had helped as much as they could, but they'd been grieving too. The days had seemed difficult for them all, even for Rosie, who had clearly noticed her mum was no longer around to snuggle with in a bed.

But it had been Rosie who got him through the worst of it. Her smile, her chuckles, her laughter. The way her eyes were exactly like her mother's, it was as if Anna still lived on, only in her daughter.

Max had found the strength to continue. His wife had made this choice for a reason. She'd told him, towards the end, that she'd never wanted to leave him alone and she had kept that promise. His desire to love and protect his daughter had driven him through every day and somehow the days had become less about survival and getting through them without crying and more about enjoying the time that they had together, as life was precious. It was a gift and you had to live in the present. Not worry about the past, or tremble at the future, because no one knew how much of that you had.

He was glad he'd told Anna's story to Bella. Because now it was in the open, it wasn't a painful secret that lurked in his past. He'd talked about it and it was done. Of course, Bella had made it so easy for him to say. There was something about her that made talking all the easier. Maybe because she'd been hurt, too? Maybe because she walked this path of single parenthood as well, and that made her a fellow traveller?

Max called his first patient of the day through. The note on the computer simply said 'numb hand'. A glance through the patient's history told him that this patient, Mary Connor, was sixty-two years of age and had been diagnosed with a tremor before, but Parkinson's tests had been negative.

Mary walked through his door with a smile and sat down in the chair beside his desk. 'Morning, Doctor! I'm Mary, pleased to meet you.' She held out her hand.

Max shook it. 'Hello. I'm Dr Moore, how can I help you today?'

'Well, it's this hand, Doctor.' She held out her

left hand. Same side as her tremor. He could see that her arm was still trembling and he'd also noticed a slight slur to her voice as she spoke. But, having never met the patient before, he didn't know if this was usual, or new. 'It feels a bit numb and my grip isn't what it used to be. I keep dropping things.'

He frowned. 'Okay, and how long has it been feeling like this?'

'A couple of weeks. Not long. I waited because I thought maybe I'd banged it and the numbness would go away, but it's not.'

'Is it getting worse? Spreading?'

'No. It's just the same.'

'And can you point out for me where the numbness is?'

Mary indicated the areas around her thumb and forefingers and near the wrist.

'And can you remember banging it?'

'No, but that doesn't mean I didn't. My husband, Tom, he says I'd forget my head if it wasn't screwed on, just lately.' Mary laughed, but he could hear behind that laughter that there was a very worried woman, trying to act as if it didn't bother her, when it clearly did.

He examined her hand, wrist and arm. Palpating it, checking the joints, rolling and flexing them, asking if anything hurt. There were no bruises that he could see. No cuts. No swelling.

But clearly she had lost sensation. He got her to try holding different things, from a thin slip of paper to a pen, to a book, and clearly her strength of grasp was lacking and the slip of paper fell to the floor instantly.

He'd been hearing the slur, more, too. 'Can I ask you, Mary, about your speech?'

'My speech?'

'Yes, I can't help but hear a bit of a slur, sometimes. Is that new, or is that something you've always had?'

She seemed to think. 'I don't know. I think it's come on in the last few months. Gradually, I think, but I've not had a stroke or anything, have I?'

'I can't rule it out at this stage. But if the slurring has been there the last few months, then it's possible that you had a mini stroke or TIA, a transient-ischaemic attack, but those don't usually leave you with symptoms. They're transient. They don't stay. Regarding your arm and hand issues… I think we need to do further tests. You also mention that your husband has noticed your memory isn't very good at the moment, so I think, if you're happy for me to do so, I'd like to refer you to a neurologist.'

'You think it's serious, then?'

'I think I'd like to rule out certain conditions, but, at this stage, it could be anything. A specialist will be able to narrow down what it is we're looking at, so that we can treat you effectively and as early as we can.'

'Right. I see. Am I going to get better?'

'I'd like to think so, but we need to do these tests to ascertain what we are working with.'

Mary looked concerned. 'I thought maybe I just had a bit of nerve damage in my old age.'

'Well, perhaps it is, but let's get you seen by someone with a more specialist knowledge, just in case.'

His patient nodded her agreement.

When she was gone, he wrote up her notes and made the referral. There was an excellent neurologist at the local hospital and he would be able to put Mary through some tests, maybe an MRI or CT scan, to ascertain what was going on. Max had seen a case like this once before, years ago, and it had turned out to be nothing but old age settling in and he hoped that this was the case here, but he had a bad feeling and he didn't like it. He knew, more than anyone else, how important it was that symptoms and diseases were caught early, so that something could be done. Even if it was for an illness that had no cure, sometimes they could slow its progression to give patients a greater quality of life, for a lot longer than they would have had if they'd left it late, or not bothered to mention it.

His next patient was a much simpler case. An obvious urine infection, for which he prescribed antibiotics. After that he saw a gentleman who thought he'd detected a lump on his testicle, but it was actually just a cyst on his cauda epididymis. A place in the testicle that stored mature sperm cells. Occasionally, this area could become filled with fluid, but it was common and often resolved itself. He checked to make sure this patient didn't have a urine infection—he didn't—and told the patient to call again if it wasn't gone by the end of the month. If it wasn't, they'd refer him for an ultrasound, just to be sure.

Max went into his morning break and cut himself a thin slice of Lorna's lemon drizzle and waited for Bella. He was looking forward to talking to her again. He felt as if she understood him. Understood the struggles of being a single parent.

But when she came into the staff area, her eyes looked red, as if she'd been crying.

Instantly, he was alarmed and got up. 'Hey, you okay?'

Bella had thought she looked okay. She'd thought all traces of her crying had to be gone.

Damn it! I waited before I came out here, too!

'I'm fine. Honestly.' She smiled, feeling embarrassed that Max had noticed. At least Lorna and Oliver weren't here too, but they'd be in Lorna's room together again, probably. 'It's nothing.'

'You're sure? Here. You sit down and I'll make you a tea. Start on my cake. I haven't touched it yet. I'll cut myself another slice.'

She eyed the cake on the low coffee table. It did look good and a hit of sugar would feel nice. She sat down and forked a mouthful of cake. It was delicious! Moist and lemony. Exactly as it ought to be.

Lorna, this is amazing.

Max handed her a mug of tea and settled opposite. 'Difficult case?'

She nodded and tried her hardest not to think about Tansy Jenkins. Or the look in her eyes. 'I don't know why some cases hit so hard. They just do. And I don't even know the young woman! I met her just this morning for the first time and have to give her the worst news in the world.'

Max nodded.

'This patient and her husband had been trying for a baby for two years. They were on the waiting list to start IVF. They even had an appointment for two months' time to start the process. Meet with a fertility specialist. But discovered they were pregnant a couple of weeks ago. But this morning, she woke up and she was bleeding and had pains, so she came to see me and…'

Bella could hear her voice tremble and, not

wanting to cry, she stopped speaking for a minute, so that she could breathe. Regain control of her voice and be professional. But it was hard sometimes as a doctor to have that emotional distance. You could try as much as you wanted but at the end of the day you were dealing with real people. And you were human, too, with empathy and sometimes the empathy won.

'I had to tell her she was probably miscarrying. Losing the most precious thing in the world to her. She couldn't stop crying. Couldn't stop blaming herself for having done a bit of gardening yesterday. Couldn't bear the idea of having to tell her husband, who'd left for work early and had no idea.' Bella let out a long breath. 'I helped her make that call. I spoke to him, too, and he cried. She cried. I cried. I mean... I was not the professional, distanced doctor that they needed in that moment.'

'You were the perfect doctor for them in that moment,' Max replied. 'You showed them that they mattered. That you cared. That they weren't just another number. Another loss. Another statistic.'

'I hope they saw it that way. But worst of all is that I felt aware of the time factor. That people in the waiting room were being kept waiting, but I couldn't do anything about that as I needed to give my patient and her husband as much time as they needed. I just felt so bad. So guilty.' Bella forked in another mouthful of lemony deliciousness and before she knew it, she'd finished the slice. Drowning her emotions with a citrus sponge cake. 'I ought to go back now, miss my break and try to catch up.' She stood to go.

Max stood with her. 'Let me take a couple off your hands.'

'Thanks, but you should take your break.'

'And so should you, after such an emotional appointment. Let me help you. Who do you have on your list?'

'A wart removal and a mole check.'

Max smiled. 'I'll take the wart, if you want.'

Bella smiled back at him. He was so kind. So thoughtful. She had completely misjudged him yesterday. He was nothing like the vain, charming Lothario she'd first imagined he might be. She'd been so unfair when she'd first met him. Judging him wrongly and all because of what had happened with Blake. She'd never have been like that before. 'Okay, thanks. You're very kind.'

'Take your tea back with you. Drink it when you can.' He passed her her drink in its mug.

She felt her fingers brush his, felt a small blush fill her cheeks at the contact. 'I will.'

They both finished work that evening at the same time, meeting each other coming out of their consultation rooms and so they headed to the infants' school to pick up Rosie and Ewan together.

Once again Bella felt extremely aware of Max at her side as they walked. He was a very handsome man and she would be lying to herself to say she wasn't attracted to him. She just knew she wouldn't act on it. She could look, but not touch. As her mum used to say, there's nothing wrong with browsing the menu, you just don't order the delicious dish.

He'd been so kind to her today. Thoughtful at her being upset, offering her his own slice of cake, taking her patients so that she didn't overrun. Little things, but they mattered. He seemed a genuinely nice guy. A gentleman. But she still felt cautious. She'd not known a single man in her life who had not let her down. Who had not lied to her. Who had not cheated, and that list included her own father. Men always wanted something and very often did not feel satisfied with what they had.

She really wanted to believe that Max was different and maybe he was, but her experience dictated to her that he wouldn't be. Somehow, he would let her down. Hurt her, if she allowed him, so that it was best to keep him at arm's length. A friend. A colleague. A neighbour. Nothing more than that.

Besides, work relationships were complicated.

Nobody wanted to mess in the company ink. And she had Ewan to think about. Ewan to be a role model for. If Bella was going to invite any man into her life, to be someone that Ewan could look up to, he had to be stellar in his behaviour. He had to be something that all men had proved to her they were not. Loyal. Honest. True. Plus Max had Rosie, he had his own worries to fret about. No. She and Max were too complicated to do anything about any attraction she might feel and that was all it was. A physical attraction. It would pass. And she didn't have to worry about it any more than that.

At the school, Ewan and Rosie came running to greet them. They'd both been playing outside on the rope bridge and even Bella noticed the difference in Max's daughter today from yesterday. Her confidence was growing and that was nice to see.

'Had a fun day?' she asked Ewan.

'Great! Me and Rosie are guinea pig monitors!'

Guinea pigs? 'Really?'

'Yes!' Rosie grinned. 'Their names are Monty and Tommy!'

'Wow.'

'We get to bring them home during the school holidays and look after them!'

'Do you?' Bella raised an eyebrow at Max, who laughed at her horrified expression. She didn't mind cats or dogs, but little things that scurried? No, sir!

'Get your bookbags, you two,' reminded the staff member of the after-school club. They'd learned her name was Lynne.

'Any problems?' Bella asked.

'None at all. Those two are really blooming and Rosie's come completely out of her shell since Ewan became her friend. He's very popular.'

Bella beamed. That was good. That was exactly what she wanted for her son.

'You can't split them up. They do everything together. It's lovely to see,' Lynne continued.

Bella couldn't help but notice that Ewan held Rosie's hand as they walked home together. It was innocent and sweet and reminded her of when she was a child and they'd gone anywhere with school, you had to hold hands with your walking partner, whether you liked them or not. She'd once had to hold hands with a young boy called Glen, who'd taken great pleasure in teasing her and pulling on her hair in assemblies. His hand had always been sweaty and she'd hated it. But Rosie and Ewan looked very happy indeed. Chattering away to one another about stuff they'd done at school that day.

She was so proud of her son. She'd spoken to him so much about this before starting school, about making sure he had friends that were girls, as much as he had friendships with boys. That he was always to be respectful and kind, no matter what, and if he ever heard his friends making fun of someone else, then he was to stop them or walk away. Bella wanted to raise a man of the future.

The lavender scent in the air added to the warm, balmy feel of the evening and they even saw, heading out of the village, Lorna and Oliver in running gear.

'I didn't know they were into running,' Max said.

'Lorna mentioned she's training for a marathon. Maybe he's helping her?' She turned to look at Max. 'What about you? Do you work out? Go to the gym?'

'Not really. I know I should, but I've always wanted to prioritise any spare time I had by spending it with Rosie, or making sure she had a relationship with Anna's parents. I've always liked walking though. Country trails, that kind of thing. I've often thought about getting a dog. I think Rosie would love it, but it wouldn't be fair on the dog to be cooped up all day.'

'*You'll* just have to make do with the school guinea pigs, then!' She laughed.

'Hmm. Not sure how I'll feel about that. But I'd imagine that would only be during school breaks. Is Ewan going to attend the after-school club during the holidays, same as Rosie? Or have you made other plans?'

'No, he'll be at the school. It seemed easiest. Less disruptive. I've got him signed up already.'

'I've done the same, too. But…how do you deal with the guilt? I'm feeling a lot of that right now.'

'I think it's to be expected. We've been their whole world for so long and then they reach four years old and suddenly we hand them off to someone else. They learn as much from their teachers and friends as they used to from us. I think it's about letting go. Accepting that this is a part of their development.'

'And do you find that easy?'

'Are you kidding me?' Bella laughed. 'I'm always worrying about Ewan getting the right messages. All I can do is give him a base to work from, but it's up to him who his friends are, which lessons he likes the best, which teachers he dislikes, how he feels he might have to change to fit in with everyone else.' She shook her head. 'I'd love to explain to him that, at school, you try your hardest to fit in and be like everyone else, because you think it's the most important thing in the world. But then, you leave school, become an adult and realise that being an individual is far, far more important and all the quirky stuff that made you stand out, or all the strange stuff you get teased for, are what make you you! And you learn to treasure it, rather than hide it. But I think he's too young for all of that.'

'Yeah.'

Bella shrugged. 'He's four. He's more interested in cartoons and animals right now.' She smiled ruefully. 'But I'll help him understand it when he's older, if there are any problems that develop.'

They reached Field Lane and began to walk up it towards their homes.

'I like talking to you,' Max said.

She smiled. Strangely, considering her feelings yesterday, she liked talking to him, too. 'Well, don't be too impressed. I only have one or two pearls of wisdom and I think I've shared them already. After this? It's all trivia and bad celebrity impressions.'

'That sounds great, too. We must get you drunk one day, so I get to see and hear them all.'

'Good luck with that.' Bella didn't drink alcohol. She'd seen how alcohol had affected her father whenever he drank, which hadn't been often, but when he had? It had been horrible. She never wanted to be that out of control. She was all Ewan had to take care of him. There was no time for getting drunk, or lying in bed. Besides, she had enough bad headaches as it was, without adding hangovers to them.

'Well, maybe one night you two should come over to ours for a pizza night. Might be fun one weekend or something? I think the kids would like it.'

Pizza? With Max and Rosie? At their cottage? The kids would love it. But was he asking her as a neighbour? A colleague? A friend? Or something else? She felt a frisson of anticipation wash over her. The thought that he might find her attractive felt quite delicious.

'Just friends,' he said, smiling. 'Obviously.'

Just friends. Obviously.

Disappointment washed over her and suddenly she felt embarrassed and silly. She was reading too much into their friendship. 'Um…this weekend?'

'How about Friday night? Come over to ours about seven p.m.? We'll do pizza, then a movie or something?'

'Okay.' She nodded, trying to control the tingles in her tummy at the idea of going over to Max's place. But it would be okay, right, because the kids would be there. No funny business would happen—*just friends, obviously*—and they'd be so close to their own home, if they had to make a rapid exit for whatever reason.

Not that there will be one, because nothing will happen.

Just friends.

Obviously.

'Great. And preference in the pizza?'

'Any kind is great.' She didn't want to seem a bother.

'Okay. It's a date. Kind of.' He frowned, then laughed. 'Rosie? Say goodbye to Ewan.'

'Bye, Ewan!' said Rosie.

'Bye, Rosie.'

She walked Ewan across the road, looking both ways before they crossed, even though Field Lane was a very quiet road and not really used except by the people who lived on it, and let Ewan into their cottage. As she turned around to close the front door, she noticed Max was waiting on his doorstep, checking to make sure they got in okay. Even though she lived only a couple of metres from his own place, he still waited to make sure she was in safely.

That's really sweet.

She gave him a smile and a quick wave and then closed the door. Bella stood there for a moment, thinking of what a nice guy Max was turning out to be, and then that evil little voice in her head that made her doubt everything spoke up.

But he's not interested in you. You've been friend-zoned. So deal with it.

* * *

Friday night had arrived and Max had managed to pick up a couple of things for pizza and movie night. He'd bought a selection of pizzas with different toppings. He'd bought popcorn for the movie and even mini ice creams for pudding, if anyone had room. He'd sorted through his extensive DVD collection and got out all the ones that Ewan might possibly choose, but, even he had to admit, Rosie's taste in movies was very rooted in princesses and fairy tales and he wasn't sure how much Ewan would like that, so he'd made sure to pop out to the Clearbrook Library at his lunchbreak that day and borrowed a range of other DVDs that might interest him.

He'd bought a bottle of wine for himself and Bella and he'd even dawdled over the flowers and wondered if he ought to buy her a bouquet. A gift of some sort. But then he'd remembered that look of fear in her eyes, when she'd thought he was asking her over as some sort of date, and so he'd forgone the flowers totally.

Not that he wouldn't have minded dating Bella if he were in a totally different situation. He liked her a lot. Being a single parent, like himself, she understood the struggles of that, but he also felt they connected on another level. This past week, with every conversation they'd had, he'd begun to like her more and more. Seeing past that beautiful exterior that she clearly wasn't aware of, to the beauty of her soul. Bella cared deeply about her job, her patients and most especially Ewan and she was doing an amazing job of raising a fabulous little boy, if Rosie's tales were anything to go by.

He wished he'd known Bella before. At medical school, the way Lorna and Oliver had known each other. He just knew, deep in his heart, that she and Anna would have loved one another and been the best of friends. They were so alike in spirit and character.

'When are they coming?' Rosie asked. She'd got changed out of her school uniform and had put on a pink tee shirt with a denim overall dress and white frilly socks.

He checked his watch. 'Any minute now, I should think. Now remember, they're our guests, so they get to choose the pizza and the movie.'

'Okay. Can I help?'

He was putting out some snacks. Crisps. Crudités. Hummus. 'Sure. Want to get the cucumber from the fridge?'

It didn't take long to finish chopping up the cucumber, carrots and putting out the mangetout. The wine was chilling nicely in the fridge, the kettle was full and he'd even managed a quick tidy. The place didn't look too bad. They'd unpacked most things, but he did still have a few boxes of Anna's things that he couldn't bring himself to get rid of. Her favourite dress. Books that she'd loved. Little bits of memorabilia. Her wedding ring. Jewellery. That he thought Rosie might like when she was older.

The doorbell rang and Rosie leapt up. 'They're here!' and she raced for the front door.

'Wait for me.' He didn't like Rosie opening the door without him there. You never knew who could be on the other side, even if you were expecting someone.

But then he was swinging the door wide and in rushed Ewan and behind him, looking awkward, but stunningly beautiful in a sun dress, was Bella. She looked completely different from how she dressed for work. This dress was very summery. Not work attire at all. It was a pale blue, with tiny daisies on it, and her hair was down and loose and he thought he could even detect some kind of perfume, which she never wore for work.

'Come in!' He stepped back and kind of held his breath as she came in. She had a diamond clip in her hair to one side and as she passed, he couldn't help but notice the long, smooth length of her neck and a hint of clavicle and he was so struck by it, he almost found himself staring and had to remind himself to close his mouth and shut the door.

Thankfully, she didn't notice him being dumb-struck by his physical reaction to her. It was disturbing to him, too. He'd not had a physical reaction to any woman since losing Anna. He'd noticed beautiful women, of course. He could appreciate them, but he'd never felt such a raw, physical disturbance at being so attracted to one.

A pang of guilt washed over him and his gaze instantly went to a picture of himself and Anna that sat on the hallway table. It was a candid shot. One that he'd always loved. Taken before they'd known she had cancer. Before she'd got pregnant. They'd gone to the seaside, despite the rain and the gloom, and had fish and chips on a beach. The picture was of them both, but in it, Anna had a cagoule hood around her face, des-perately trying to keep the rain off, and she'd been laughing heartily and he'd quickly snapped it with his phone to capture the moment.

It was the last time they'd ever been to the seaside. The last time they'd ever gone away to-gether. Weeks later, she'd fallen pregnant and the whole cancer nightmare had begun.

Max closed the door and followed Bella and Ewan into the kitchen. Rosie had already invited Ewan to go and play in the garden and the two kids had disappeared out of the back door.

'I brought you this.' Bella smiled and passed him a small gift bag.

'Oh! You didn't have to bring anything.'

'It's just a small thank you for inviting us over.'

He opened the bag and found a small box of ornate, but very expensive chocolates. 'Wow. Thank you. That's very kind.' He pondered about whether he should lean in to give her a thank-you peck on the cheek, but after what he'd felt in the hallway? He wasn't sure he wanted to feel any more guilt and so he simply smiled and said, 'Wine?'

'I don't drink, but tea would be lovely.'

'Tea, it is.' He smiled again, broader this time, and started to make them both a cup of tea. 'You'd think those two would be exhausted after a long day, wouldn't you?'

Bella laughed. 'I think kids have different fuel packs from adults. When do we lose it, do you think? That endless energy?'

'Erm…when responsibilities begin to weigh us down?'

'Maybe. Can I help with anything?'

'It's all done. Why don't you take a seat? Or would you like a tour of the place?'

'A tour would be great!'

Max gave her a quick tour of the cottage. It didn't take long—it was only two-bedroomed. But apparently, his place was nothing like hers, even though they looked the same from the outside. Her kitchen had a separate, smaller dining area, whereas his was combined, but upstairs, she thought that maybe her bedroom was bigger and it had an en suite, whereas he had a separate dressing area.

Back in the kitchen, he stood by the back door and asked the kids what kind of pizza they wanted. They settled on ham and pineapple and whilst it was in the oven he set about making a home-made coleslaw.

'Have you always liked to cook?' Bella asked.

'I learned to. I'm afraid I was your typical barbecue man, standing over the fire in my pinny and tongs cooking sausages, until Anna got sick. Then she didn't have the energy and so I learned to cook and found I rather enjoyed it. What about you?'

'I love food, don't get me wrong, but I actually hate the whole business of cooking. The end result is wonderful, but I hate all that cleaning up you have to do. How much mess it makes, how much extra work it creates. What I need in my life is a personal chef and kitchen maid, then I'd be happy.'

'I think we all would be!' he agreed, smiling.

'Staff. I think I just need staff. To be honest, I thought working full time in a job at last and not being a locum would feel so good, and it does, but I hadn't taken into account how exhausted

I'd feel at the end of each day. I just want to flop on the sofa, yet there's cleaning to do, cooking, shopping, laundry, spending quality time with Ewan. Making sure he's bathed before bed, reading him a story. It's a lot, you know?'

'You need me time. Time to recharge?'

'Yes! Oh, listen to me! I never thought I'd complain about being a mum and having a great job, yet here I am.' She sounded embarrassed and he didn't want her to feel that way.

'You're human and there are only so many hours in the day. It's natural and you're *not* complaining. Just stating facts. I feel the same sometimes. When do we find time for friends? For ourselves? Going out? Visiting family? It all comes at a cost. A cost of time and energy. We're allowed to feel like we're flagging at some point, when there's just one of us holding down the fort. Other people have partners to share the load, remember?' He placed the bowl of freshly prepared coleslaw on the table and got out the salad he'd made with Rosie earlier, from the fridge.

'You're right.'

Ewan and Rosie came bursting through the back door then, full of smiles.

'Go wash your hands, you two. Pizza will be ready in two minutes.'

Rosie grabbed Ewan's hand and pulled him towards a bathroom.

'I love how easy they are together. It's like they've known one another for ages.'

'They have. A whole week!'

Bella smiled.

He liked her smile. The way it lit her eyes. The way her cheeks rounded. The softness of her lips.

I must stop focusing on her lips!

But it was difficult not to. Especially when he liked to make her smile, too. It made him feel good. It made him feel as if he was doing something right. He used to try so hard to make Anna smile when she was going through treatment, but she'd felt so ill and so weak most days, it had been difficult. He'd felt as though he was failing her. Rosie had been able to make his wife smile. Or maybe she'd just saved her strength for her daughter? When he'd sat by Anna's bedside and reminisced with her, trying to make her remember happier times, he'd smiled himself and held her hand and tried to make her comfortable and fetched her whatever she'd needed.

So, yes, he felt good that he could make Bella smile and he told himself not to feel guilty about doing so. He'd been starved of it for so long.

Her happiness made him feel better about himself and that was worth its weight in gold.

They'd had a lovely evening together. Bella couldn't remember the last time she'd been at a friend's house with her son, laughing so hard and just enjoying another person's company. These last few difficult years as she'd struggled to raise Ewan on her own, she'd often felt isolated and alone. So, to be invited out, to be asked to bring Ewan along, to sit and watch some silly cartoon movie about anthropomorphised cars, whilst eating the most delicious pizza—had been wonderful.

She knew the evening had to draw to a close when Ewan couldn't stop yawning. It was nearing nine o'clock at night and it was a whole hour past his usual bedtime. There'd be no time for a bath before bed, but she figured she could let it go for one night.

'All right. Time for bed, you,' she said, stroking his thick mop of hair.

'Can we stay a little longer, Mummy, please?' Ewan begged.

She considered it. But a brief look at Rosie and she could see that Max's daughter had tired eyes too, and she didn't want to outstay their welcome, even though she also didn't want to bring this brilliant time together to an end. Because once she got back home and Ewan was in bed, she'd be alone again.

'I think we all need to get some rest. Come on!'

They got up and headed to the front door,

thanking Max and Rosie profusely for having them over and welcoming them to their home.

'You're very welcome! We've loved every minute of it and we must do it again.'

She found herself agreeing. 'Absolutely! But you must come over to ours next time.'

'Sounds like a plan,' Max agreed, opening the door as Ewan gave Rosie a hug goodbye.

Seeing her son hug Rosie, Bella figured that she ought to thank Max, too, in a similar way. It would be harmless, right? A hug, a peck on the cheek from a friend, that was all. But she felt herself blushing as she leaned in to give him a quick hug, felt a heat suffuse her body at the feel of him taking her in his arms, and when she pressed her lips to his cheek? Felt the brief brush of bristles against her own skin? She felt alarm at how much she wanted to stay there. Within his grasp. With his hands still upon her.

Bella pulled away, blushing. 'Well, thanks again. Goodnight.'

'Goodnight.'

She blew out a breath as she and Ewan crossed the street to their own cottage and once again she couldn't help but notice that Max didn't close his front door until she'd gone inside and closed her own.

He'd given her one last beaming smile and a

wave and she'd waved back, feeling her heart thumping madly in her chest.

Something was happening here between her and Max. Was it just friendship? It felt that way and she wasn't sure where all these other feelings were coming from. He'd given her no sign he wanted anything else and yet her mind was awhirl.

She'd so fiercely kept herself away from men since the break-up with Blake. Had told herself that she would remain single for ever now, until her dying day, because she could never imagine trusting a man ever again. And yet here she was, developing feelings for Max. A guy!

The stress of it all was bringing on another headache. She rubbed at her forehead and looked at herself in the hall mirror as Ewan headed upstairs to brush his teeth before bed.

I look tired. Are those bags I'm getting?

She rubbed at her face and let out a heavy sigh, before kicking off her shoes and heading upstairs to hopefully read Ewan a very short story before he'd fall asleep.

Bella thought about what it must feel like to be a parent if you could share the burden with someone else. She pictured putting Ewan to bed. Then Rosie, and going downstairs to find Max on her sofa. How she'd sink into his welcoming arms and they'd snuggle. Watch a bit of television, before suggesting they go to bed themselves. Watching him undress. Feeling the mattress sink as he got in beside her. The warmth of his long, hard body pressed up against hers as they spooned. The feel of his hand gently stroking down her side, smoothing over her hip, sliding up her thigh...

But what if it wasn't all it was cracked up to be? Like on social media where everyone always posted pics and videos of their amazing, happy lives. It wasn't always like that. It couldn't be. Behind the scenes there were probably arguments and upsets. Strained silences. Betrayals.

It couldn't be perfect. She might envy couples who could share the load, but did she envy them everything else? The wondering if the late night at work meant something else? Whether taking his phone outside meant he was having a call with someone he shouldn't? Whether the flowers he brought home really were for the fact that he simply loved her?

Max seemed wonderful.

Perfect.

But would that all change if they took their relationship beyond friendship?

She had to accept that it could.

But she couldn't accept the risk that it might...

CHAPTER FOUR

MAX HAD RACHEL and baby Hayden back in his clinic first thing for her check-up since she'd seen him last time for possible postnatal depression. When she came into his room, she looked just as hassled and just as pale as she had done before.

'How's the past few days been?'

'Difficult, if I'm honest. I'm still not sleeping great and Hayden is still colicky. It got really bad a couple of nights ago. I had to hand him off to my husband and go into another room, just to gather myself.'

'So you've spoken to your husband about the difficulties you've been having?'

She nodded. 'He's trying to understand, but I'm not sure that he does. He's smitten with Hayden. Perfect with him. Hayden doesn't cry as much for him. It's like he's better at being a parent than me.' Rachel began to cry and he passed her the tissue box, letting her cry, letting her get out this frustration that she was feeling.

'I just feel so sad all the time. It never goes away and I feel like I'm failing my baby.'

This most definitely was not baby blues. This tiredness, guilt, sadness that Rachel was feeling, all pointed to a case of postnatal depression. He was so glad that Anna had never had to go through this, too.

'I just…wake every day and before I even open my eyes, I feel this sense of doom. Like this thought going round and round in my head of how on earth am I going to get through the day, today? I've stopped going out. I avoid people. I don't answer the phone, because everyone expects me to be happy.'

Max nodded. 'I understand. And I think it's really important that we get you feeling better. I'd like to refer you to a counselling service. They can come to your home, if you can't make it out and about, though I think they prefer it if you can try and make it to them. I'd also like to prescribe an antidepressant to help with your mood. How do you feel about doing that?'

'Fine. I need to feel better. I can't keep going on like this.'

'It's important for me to ask though, Rachel. Have you ever had any thoughts of harming yourself, or Hayden?'

She looked shocked. 'No! I'd never!'

'Okay.' He smiled soothingly. 'I had to ask.

Now there's no shame in having postnatal depression. It affects at least one in ten women after birth. It's not a weakness. It doesn't mean something is wrong with you and we don't know why it affects some women and not others. Do you write a diary or a journal?'

'I used to.'

'Do you think you could keep one? Maybe write in it each day about how you've felt? Maybe have a mood tracker? You can download various templates from the Internet. But try to keep track of your mood and emotions daily. It will help to spot some triggers and will also help the counsellor that sees you.'

'All right.'

'The important thing to understand right now is that this is treatable. And it is temporary. You *will* start to feel better and it might help to write that on the first page, so that every time you open your notebook or journal, you see that.'

'Okay. That sounds a good idea.'

'Now, I know you're breastfeeding, so I'm going to prescribe a medicine that will not pass through the breast milk, so it will be totally safe for you to take.'

Rachel nodded. 'Okay.'

'And I want you to try and get outside for a walk every day if you feel you can manage that. Fresh air and exercise will help you, and I want you to take this leaflet.' He passed her a leaflet from his desk. 'It lists all the places where you can get help, and that one on the bottom? Puts you in touch with another mother who's been through the same thing. Like a buddy, or sponsor.'

'That sounds helpful.'

'It can take the antidepressants a few weeks to start working, so shall I see you again in about two weeks? See how you're doing? But again, if you feel you need to be seen sooner, or things get worse in any way, you call immediately, okay?'

'Thank you, Dr Moore. You've been very kind and understanding.'

'It all just takes a little time, okay? But everyone, me, your husband, your health visitor, your family, they all want the best for you and we're all here to listen and to help. This isn't a burden you should feel you're shouldering alone.'

Her eyes welled up at that, but she simply nodded, thanked him again and left. Max wished there were a magic button he could push to make her see that the clouds would lift. That would improve her mood and make her feel connected with her baby. He hoped she wouldn't look back on this period and hate the fact that she missed out on enjoying her son's early weeks. But there was no magic button. If there were, he would have pressed it a long time ago, to take away his wife's cancer because, by rights, she should have been here to enjoy Rosie. To see the beautiful young girl she had grown into. He wasn't meant to be alone, either. They were supposed to be on this parenthood road together. That was the deal.

His mind drifted to Bella and Ewan.

When they'd come round for pizza and a movie, had been wonderful. Sitting there, in the dark, laughing, enjoying the film. It had felt like family. Had given him a taste of what could have been.

I wonder if Bella felt the same way, too?

Them getting up to go had broken the spell. Left him wanting.

And then, when Bella had kissed him goodbye on the cheek? He'd felt a pull. Wanted more. Wanted to hold onto her and never let go. To squeeze her tight. To breathe her in.

To not feel alone any more.

He'd honestly not realised how lonely he'd been lately. He'd thought he was fine. Him and Rosie against the world.

But there was so much that he missed. So much that he needed.

Could he find that with Bella? He knew she liked him, but that was as friends and neighbours and colleagues. And it wouldn't be simple for either of them. They were both single parents, they each had a responsibility to their child first. And what if he asked for more and she wasn't willing to give it? How would that affect them at work? How would that affect their friendship, if Bella knew he'd wanted more, but she wasn't ready to give it? Bella had been cheated on. She'd be wary, he knew that. So was he. He'd had his heart broken in the worst possible way and he wasn't sure he could go through something like that again. No. He could never go through that again. He'd already made so many sacrifices in his life, he would not do so again. They would have to remain friends.

He went to the staffroom to fill up his water bottle and noticed a leaflet on the side for a travelling fair that was coming to just outside Clearbrook. It would be a lovely place to take Rosie. Every child should go to a funfair at least once.

He couldn't help but think, *I wonder if Bella and Ewan would like to go, too?*

Bella was saying goodbye to a patient who'd been in to see her and walked out with a diagnosis of tennis elbow, or lateral epicondylitis, to give it its clinical name, when Max caught her attention as he was heading to his consultation room. He held a leaflet in his hand.

'Just saw this. Fancy taking the kids to it?'

She took the leaflet and saw *Lawton's Family Fair! Coming Soon!* The fair seemed to promise fun rides, inflatables, games, hot food and drinks and the admission prices seemed pretty reasonable too. 'It's this weekend.'

'Looks fun. What do you think?'

'Can I think about it? Check my diary?' she asked.

'Sure. Let me know.' And he gave her a smile and disappeared into his room.

Bella did not need to check her diary. She knew her weekend was clear. Her weekends were always clear, because they were the days she dedicated to Ewan and Ewan would *love* to go to the fair!

But she did need to think about it. Her headaches were still bad and she imagined that at the fair there'd be lots of loud music pumping from speakers at various stalls. There'd be flashing lights and strong smells and that wouldn't help any. But the biggest thing she felt was wariness. Fear. Doubt. Last Friday, they'd met up for pizza night. Somehow, she'd offered to host next time.

Next time? What am I doing?

Going to the fair together? Was it too much? Were they doing too many things together? They already walked to school together every day. Often went to pick up the kids together—only one night had one of them had a heavier admin load than the other and that had been that first night. When Bella had met Rosie in the after-school club.

Would he read too much into it?

Will I?

Because the more time she spent in Max's company, the more she found herself stealing glances. Wondering what he was thinking. What he thought of her. What it might feel like to kiss him. What it might feel like to not be a single parent and not have issues with trust and how crazy it would be to throw caution to the wind and just pull him towards her and kiss him so passionately that the rest of the world would disappear.

She had crazy flights of fancy like that.

Who wouldn't with a guy like Max?

Bella couldn't believe she was even considering it. Going with him to the fair. Max was dangerous. A threat to her emotional well-being, because he was so easy to like. So warm. She'd not got involved with anyone since Blake and she'd seriously believed that she never would again. But here she was. Thinking about saying yes.

I'm probably reading too much into it anyway! He's just a single parent, like me, looking to take his kid somewhere fun, and he knows how much Ewan would enjoy it, too.

Bella looked down at the leaflet. Was she even

seriously considering keeping Ewan away from this, just so that no one else got the wrong idea about what was happening between them? She'd always tried to make the best decisions for her son and he'd never been to a funfair before. And she would not keep him away from this. Imagine him going to school and discovering all his friends had been and he had not?

I'm sure I'm perfectly capable of staying away from Max. I've had years of practice of keeping myself apart from guys.

Bella found herself standing outside Max's door. She rapped her knuckles against the wood.

'Come in!'

She opened the door and wafted the leaflet in front of him. 'I checked my diary and we can go. When's best for you?'

His smile, when it broke across his face, made her feel good. Clearly, she'd made him very happy indeed. 'How about the Sunday afternoon? If we go about two o'clock? That should give us a couple of hours there and have them both home in time for tea, bath and bed at a reasonable hour before school the next day.'

She gave a nod. 'Sounds like a plan. Two o'clock it is.'

'Can't wait.'

Bella smiled and closed his door, letting out a breath. She didn't understand why she was so worked up about this. Why did it feel as if it were a date? Because it wasn't. A date usually involved just two consenting adults—they didn't bring their kids along.

Or maybe they do, if they're single parents?

Bella had no idea. She'd never done this before. Dating Blake had seemed much easier. Simpler. They'd gone to pubs and restaurants. Once they'd even gone to see a show in London at the West End. Blake had turned up at her house with a stretch limo once and taken her to a ball. That had been an amazing night. A night she could spend proudly on his arm. Feeling the eyes of everyone on them as they'd arrived. The way he'd held her hand as she'd alighted from the car. He'd been so wonderful to her in those early weeks of their courtship. He'd been wonderful for what she'd thought was years, until she'd realised it had all been a hoax and that he'd completely pulled the wool over her eyes.

She'd been so blind and she didn't want to make the same mistakes again. Wouldn't let any dashing charmer humiliate her like that again. And though she felt in her heart that Max wouldn't do that, she'd believed the same thing once about Blake.

Was there any way to be sure? To know?

All I can do is be sensible, and if I feel that

this thing begins to run away with me, then I'll just have to be strong enough to put a stop to it.

Bella nodded to herself and began working through a referral to physio for her last patient.

The Lawton Family Funfair was situated in a couple of farmer's fields just outside Clearbrook.

Rosie and Ewan were getting so excited and they hadn't even got there yet, but as they parked up they could hear the loud music being blasted from large speakers and the lavender scent that usually pervaded the air was taken up instead by the twin aromas of fried onions and candy floss.

Families, couples, groups of kids were all making their way along the road towards the fair, the entranceway marked by an arch of lights and a clown figure holding a big bunch of helium balloons shaped like cartoon characters and superheroes.

'What do you fancy going on first?' Max asked Rosie, who was holding his hand.

Rosie shrugged, uncertain.

But Ewan, who was raring to go, said, 'Everything!'

Max turned to Bella and laughed. 'I think it's going to be an expensive afternoon for you!'

She nodded. 'Tell me about it.'

As they passed the clown, they headed into a line of game stalls. Hook a duck. Another where you could try and throw ping-pong balls into goldfish bowls. Another where you could throw darts at playing cards. A coconut shy. A shooting range. A basketball net. All the stallholders happily called out to attract newcomers to part with their cash. Beyond them, they saw rides—teacups, a small carousel, a ghost train, a big wheel. Horns blared, music blasted, people screamed and laughed.

Max felt Rosie cling more tightly to him. 'Shall we try to hook a duck?' he said, kneeling down to be on her level.

She nodded and he paid for them all to have a go. It was quite easy to hook a duck, but only ducks with odd numbers on the bottom would win a prize and they had no idea how many ducks actually had those. Max hooked a duck with an even number, as did Ewan and Rosie, but Bella selected a duck with the number seven on it and got to choose a prize from the shelf of cuddly toys. Bella smiled at Ewan and said, 'You pick one.'

Ewan eyed the soft toys. 'Rosie can pick.'

Rosie pointed at a pink teddy bear no bigger than her hand and Bella gave it to her. 'Here you go!'

Rosie beamed. 'Thank you!'

Max smiled, too. That was so thoughtful of Ewan and her to do that.

His daughter clung to her teddy and his hand as they reached the teacups. 'Can we go on this, Daddy?'

'Absolutely.' He and Rosie climbed into one teacup, Bella and Ewan the next. It was so nice to see the kids' faces so lit up with joy and happiness. As the music played and he showed Rosie how to turn the cups, gently, because he didn't want her to feel ill, he couldn't help but glimpse Bella and Ewan in theirs, next to them, and Ewan was spinning them like crazy! Bella's face was an absolute picture and he couldn't help but laugh out loud. When the ride stopped, he held his hand out to her, to help her out of the teacup, and she took his hand in hers with relief.

'Thank you!'

'You're welcome.' And he realised, in that moment, that he didn't actually want to let go of her hand. Only he had to. Guiltily, he let go, but it was as if he could still feel her hand in his. As if the imprint of it were seared into his memory. He tried not to think too hard about it. Tried to lose himself in watching Rosie ride the carousel. Taking pictures of her each time she came around, capturing her happiness for ever in an image that would later become his next screensaver.

Bella took Ewan on the ghost train, but Rosie didn't fancy that one, so they waited for them, watching them disappear through two doors that hooted and hollered ghost noises, as sirens blared and horns hooted and they eventually came blasting through two black doors on the other side, looking exhilarated and happy.

'Again! Again!' yelled Ewan.

'Maybe later.' Bella laughed, clambering out of the car.

They stopped briefly to get hot dogs for them all and they sat down at a set of benches to eat their food. They were delicious. Frankfurters on long, fluffy, white finger rolls, covered with caramelised onions and drizzled with tomato sauce and mustard. They all must have been really hungry, because everyone ate every bite. After, they played at a few more stalls. Ewan won a yo-yo that whistled, Max won his daughter another teddy and Bella won a stuffed dog after knocking over a pile of cans with little bean bags.

'Mummy, can we go on the big wheel?' Ewan asked.

'I guess. How about you guys?' Bella looked to him and Rosie.

'Why not?'

They got into the queue and that was when Ewan said, 'Can Rosie and me go in one and you two go in another?'

Max looked at Bella with one eyebrow raised. Alone in a big wheel? It did have pods designed for little kids interspersed with larger ones for adults and there was a sign at the bottom saying that it was safe. 'What do you say, Rosie?'

She nodded.

'Okay,' Bella said. 'But you must behave yourself with Rosie. No swinging the pod and scaring her. You hear me?'

'I won't.'

'Cross your heart.'

Ewan mimed crossing his heart.

'We'll be in the pod behind you, so we'll see if you do!' Bella warned.

He trusted her and he trusted Ewan. So far, Bella's son had looked out for Rosie at school and so he was also going to trust him here. Rosie did, too, so this was going to be a big test for them all.

But the last week or so had shown Max that he could leave his daughter to be looked after and protected by someone else and if Rosie felt confident about it, then so would he.

They watched and waited patiently as the previous riders disembarked and then, pod by pod, they loaded up. Rosie and Ewan got into a red pod, with white stars on it, the door clanking shut behind them as they took their seats and got strapped in. Then their pod moved forward and he and Bella stepped into a blue pod that had big white polka dots on it and he couldn't help it, but he kind of felt a little nervous. Sitting this close to her, in such a confined space. Just the two of them.

The pod had open windows either side and they could hear the music being piped in, as slowly they began to ascend. Ahead of them, they could see Ewan and Rosie waving to people as they got higher and higher.

'This is amazing,' Bella said. 'I don't think I've ever been on a big wheel before.'

He was surprised and turned to look at her. 'You haven't?'

'No. Have you?'

'A long time ago. With friends. But I have to admit that we were maybe a little too drunk to have appreciated it properly. My friend, Matty, kept trying to roll the pod and thought it was hilarious. By the time we got off, I was almost ill.'

She laughed. 'Are you still in touch?'

'Sometimes. He's an army doctor, so I occasionally get a postcard or two. Oh, my God, look at that! Doesn't Clearbrook look amazing from up here?' The pod had risen above the fair, higher into the sky, and now they could see across the fields, past the lavender farms, towards the village. It looked picture-postcard perfect. Thatched roofs, and quaint roads dotted by colourful flowers, and the north side of the village, flanked by huge fields of purple lavender.

It was almost romantic.

'It looks amazing! Where's Field Lane? Can we see our cottages from here?'

Max had to lean over her way to look out of Bella's window to check. Trying to orient himself from the sky, like a bird, was weird, but eventually he worked out which road was theirs. 'There, see? By that big oak tree, over to the left?'

She nodded, turning to him, smiling. 'I see it.'

And that was when he realised that he was mere inches from her face. Her smiling, happy face. Her beautiful, gorgeous face. Her mouth. Her lips. This woman whom he had only just begun to know. Whom he worked with every day. Who seemed to adore his daughter, just as much as he did. This beautiful soul. He felt himself staring at her, hesitant, afraid to make a move, but considering one.

She looked back at him, realising the intent in his gaze.

And if he'd thought for any moment, that she did not want him to kiss her, he would not have done so. But she didn't look that way. She looked…breathless, apprehensive, yes, but…as if she was ready to try a kiss, too.

It shocked him. Surprised him, but the look in her eyes told him that he could do this and, feeling emboldened, he leaned in a little further, their lips millimetres apart. One last bit of eye contact. One last check that this was okay, that she gave her consent—that was incredibly important to him—and it was all he could think of. All the other stuff between them was forgotten. That this was his co-worker. That this was his neighbour. That this was his good friend. That was all gone. All that mattered, in that intimate moment, was the fact that he wanted, needed, to kiss her. To see how it felt. To see how she tasted.

The sounds of the funfair were gone. The aromas. The rest of the world. All there was were him and her, pressed tightly together in that pod. Her mouth near his. Her lips parted in expectation.

He pressed a hand to the side of her face and leaned in for the kiss.

For a moment, he was lost. Fireworks could have gone off, bombs could have exploded and he wouldn't have noticed, because all that mattered was her. The feel of her. Her softness. The way she gently kissed him back, losing herself, too, the way her tongue gently caressed his and then was gone again. The heat that flared in his body, the way his body stirred in response to her touch, her taste, her softness and suddenly, they were breaking apart and staring into each other's eyes and looking shocked at each other. At what had just happened. At what they had both just felt.

CHAPTER FIVE

MAX DIDN'T KNOW whether to apologise, or to make a joke, or to say nothing. He didn't want to break the spell, he didn't want the pod to reach the ground and put them back into the real world again. The real world had been suspended whilst they were in the pod, isolated, in their own self-made world, where there was nothing but each other.

He wanted to kiss her again. To try it again, to see if the second time would feel just as magical as the first.

And then, before he could say anything, they were at the bottom of the ride and the big-wheel guy was clanking open their pod and he stepped out and there were Rosie and Ewan waiting for them and he scooped his daughter up into his arms.

'Did you enjoy that?' It seemed easier to pretend that nothing had happened right there and then. The kids hadn't seen, it would have been impossible for them to have seen, and if he pretended everything was normal, then maybe it would be and he would realise that he hadn't made a huge mistake and risked their friendship, or anything like that.

'You could see the whole world!' Rosie exclaimed.

Max smiled and kissed his daughter's cheek. He glanced at Bella, feeling a little embarrassed. A little guilty. How was she feeling? But she was kneeling down, away from him, straightening her son's collar on his jacket and smiling as Ewan babbled on about a bird they'd seen fly past.

Maybe the whole world could stay the same.

Maybe they could pretend the kiss hadn't happened.

Because miracles happened, right?

They had to.

They just had to.

What madness had overtaken him to do such a thing? They could have carried on as they always had, but an impulsiveness had overtaken him, because of what? The way her eyes had looked in the shadow of the pod? The proximity?

No. It was more than that. They weren't strangers, they'd slowly become friends, and he had come to look forward to every walk to school each morning and after work. He'd gone to her house this Friday just gone, her turn, she'd said, and he'd had a wonderful time. The kids had sat at a table completing a jigsaw puzzle together and he and Bella had sat next to each other on the couch, talking, laughing, sharing stories. *Bonding.*

And he'd realised that he really, really liked her. How much they had in common. She'd shown him some of her paintings that she'd done. Mostly watercolour, and she was talented. She'd been most self-deprecating and couldn't see her own talent, but she had it. There was even a huge canvas above her fireplace of a watercolour that she'd done of a giant amaryllis flower and it was stunningly beautiful. Graceful, light of touch, the pinks and yellows flowing into each other seamlessly.

He'd noticed his hand just inches away from hers and he'd had to pull it away, because the temptation to reach out and fold her hand within his had been too much. Instead, he'd laughed to himself, embarrassed, frozen, and he'd stood up as if to examine the painting more intensely, but in reality he'd needed to get away from her, to stop himself from touching her. From reaching out to feel her skin against his.

The kids had been oblivious to the tension. Had Bella? His body hadn't felt like his own, so he'd shoved his hands into his jeans pockets where they'd been safe and unlikely to reach out without his permission. But then she'd got up from the sofa and come to stand beside him and she'd begun to talk about how she'd painted the amaryllis and all he could do had been stare at her profile and gaze at her lips and her eyes and the way her dark hair fell about her shoulders and he'd known he couldn't stay a moment longer. Because if he had? Something would have happened. He would not have been able to stop himself.

As he hadn't on the big wheel.

Getting in the big-wheel pod with Max had felt unnerving, because it would be the first time the two of them would be together, hidden away from the world, in an enclosed space. They were together at work, but there were always other colleagues around and they had a job to do and of course they were professionals. When they were walking the kids to school, Ewan and Rosie were there. Walking to school together to pick up the kids at the end of the day? They were out in public and she felt relatively at ease.

But getting into that pod?

At first, she had been incredibly nervous. Her stomach dancing with butterflies and her blood pulsing through her ears louder than the music that had been blaring from the speakers, or so it had seemed. But then she'd begun to relax as they'd marvelled at how the fair and Clearbrook looked so beautiful from such a height. It had been like looking down on a cute model village and the lights from the fair had sparkled and dazzled and, for a moment, it had felt as though they were in another world!

They'd tried to spot their own cottages and Max had leaned across to point and something had shifted. Whether it had been the press of him up against her, or the way the multitudes of light had been reflecting off his face, but she'd suddenly found that she couldn't stop staring at him. Marvelling at his broad smile, feeling the attraction for him well up and spill over whatever walls she'd put up to protect herself from this very kind of thing.

It had almost been like not having control over her own body—it had simply reacted to him. She might have told her mind that she would never allow anything to happen with Max, but it was as if the rest of her hadn't got that memo.

She liked Max. A lot. He was funny. Charming. Handsome. Kind. A great dad and, yes, even though she'd only known him for a short period of time, she'd begun to think of him as a wonderful new friend.

And that kiss...

Wow. I mean... I cannot deal!

His kiss had been tender, yet passionate. Intense and yet gentle. He'd cradled her face and she had felt her heart melt, being made to feel as if she were something precious, something fragile, something that he cherished, because she'd not been made to feel that way for a long time.

When had she last had anything, or experienced anything, that was uniquely just for her? That had nothing to do with being a mum, or a doctor, or a friend? That kiss had been something special and that kiss had also changed everything, because when they'd breathlessly broken apart, she'd not known what to say. And he'd looked at her as if he'd been just as shocked at what had happened and he'd even looked a little guilty.

Of course. The last woman he probably kissed like that was Anna.

And he felt bad.

I'm the other woman still, even though his wife is dead.

She sensed his regret and it made her clam up and so the second the pod revolved to the floor and the door was opened, she got out as quickly as she could to make sure the kids were okay and fuss with Ewan's top, and asked him if he needed the loo, or whether he wanted to go home yet.

Bella hoped and prayed that Ewan *would* want to go home. Because she needed some space.

Some time to breathe and process what had just happened between herself and Max.

Would they be able to ignore it, then? Pretend it never happened? That would be easiest, wouldn't it?

Ewan yawned. 'I want to stay.'

'Hmm. You look tired.'

I'm shaking. Look at my hands trembling!

'I think we ought to make a move,' she said, louder, for the benefit of Max, who she could not bring herself to look at yet. She didn't want to see the regret in his eyes again. Clearly he wasn't ready for anything else.

'You're going? I'll drive us back.'

Damn. She'd forgotten that they'd come out here in his car. 'No! You stay and enjoy yourselves, we'll walk, or grab a taxi.' Finally she managed to look at him. Briefly, but she managed eye contact. She could see he looked pained and interpreted it as apology. He'd not meant to kiss her. It was a mistake. Of course it was a mistake!

And here she was again, feeling hurt because of a guy.

I knew I should have kept my distance!

'No. Let me drive you,' Max insisted.

So she let him drive them home. As usual, the two kids chatted away quite happily in the back seat of the car, but up front it was uncomfortably quiet. When he parked up in Field Lane, he turned to her. 'Bella, I—'

She pushed open the car door and got out, without waiting to hear what he was going to say. 'Thanks for the lift.' She helped Ewan out, let him say goodbye to Rosie and then they were marching across the road to their own cottage.

This time, she didn't turn to check if he was waiting to make sure she got inside safely. She didn't turn at all. Not even to wave to Rosie, which she felt bad about. She just wanted to get indoors and hide.

And breathe.

And *think*.

Too easily she'd allowed herself to get close to another guy. Why had she allowed it to happen? Because they worked together? Because they were both single parents with kids in the same class, who lived opposite one another? It was hardly the basis for a relationship now, was it? She'd let herself be taken in by a handsome guy, again. And she'd felt his rejection of her, almost instantly, when she'd seen the regret of his actions in his eyes.

I'm a fool!

How on earth was she going to face him tomorrow on the walk to school? The entire day at work?

How would she ever face him again?

* * *

When Max woke the next day, after a night of stunted and disturbed sleep, his stomach was a bundle of nerves. He'd wanted to try to explain to Bella how he felt, how he didn't want anything to change between them, but she'd not given him the chance.

Not in front of the kids anyway and he could respect that, so maybe at work today, they could talk? He hoped that he would give her the chance to talk. Maybe after they'd dropped the kids off at school and on their way to the practice?

He let Rosie knock on Bella's door. Max stood out on the lane and waited, holding Rosie's book-bag and PE kit that she needed that day.

Bella and Ewan came out and he looked at her to try and gauge how she was feeling. She managed a tight smile at him. 'Morning.'

'Morning.'

He hated that he'd made her feel any particular way. He didn't want her to feel bad about this. This was something that he had done. She was not in any way to blame for anything.

The kids ran ahead and he unexpectedly got some alone time with her.

'How are you?'

'Good. I'm good. How are you?' she asked, looking at anything that wasn't him.

'Fine. Listen…about yesterday…'

She stopped walking, turned to face him. 'Let's just forget about it. Let's just forget it ever happened and we'll just move on, okay?' Her voice sounded bright. As if she was trying to convince herself as much as she was trying to convince him.

'If that's what you want?' He felt hurt, even though he wanted them to move on and pretend everything was normal, too. Hurt because he'd felt something during that kiss. Something that had disturbed him so greatly that it had almost caused him to be mute. He'd not expected such a strong connection, had not expected to feel so much for Bella, this soon. How long had they known each other? Was it possible to feel this much for someone so quickly?

Of course, he'd heard of people who reportedly fell in love at first sight. Or couples who said they just knew the second they met their person. Or couples who moved in with one another after a week and were still together forty-odd years later, with children and grandchildren. But they were all *stories*.

Stuff like that had never happened to him. Even with Anna, who'd he'd believed to be the one and only love of his life, ever.

It was the shock of what he'd felt for Bella in that kiss, in that moment in which the world had paused, that had stunned him into silence. That had caused him to realise that he'd been wrong about that prior belief.

'It is. We'll just carry on like it never happened, okay?'

'Okay.' It wasn't okay. Not really. But if she wasn't willing to explore this, then maybe she thought the kiss was a horrendous mistake. And he had to respect her wishes. He wasn't sure how he was going to be able to tell himself that he could not pursue this, but he would. Somehow. Having her as his friend, neighbour, colleague, would be enough, right? It wasn't as though she was going to walk away and disappear from his life. He needed her. Wanted her, by his side as all of those things. His connection to Bella was so strong already and it grew every day and there was nothing he could do about it. And he'd nearly ruined it with an impulsive act.

They dropped the kids off and began their walk to work. It was a beautiful day and the lavender scent filled the air again and Bella chatted on about endless things—the weather, the flowers in people's gardens, how beautiful the ginger cat was that they often saw here sitting on a low stone wall.

He would smile. Nod. Occasionally answer in monosyllabic words. But he wanted to say so much more. He felt as if he might burst if he couldn't fully apologise for his actions. If he couldn't explain properly what had happened. But that was his fault. He was the one that had kissed her, not the other way around, and if this was how she chose to deal with this, then he would go along with it.

When they got to work, Lorna was just coming out of the bathroom, having changed into her work clothes after running in. They both said hello to her and then Bella grabbed a mug of tea and disappeared into her room.

'Everything okay with Bella?' Lorna asked.

'Er.... Yeah, I think so. Why?'

'I don't know, she just seemed a little unsettled.'

'No. Everything's fine.'

'Well, I might pop my head around her door. Check on her, just in case.'

He smiled, wondering if Bella would confide in Lorna about what had happened yesterday.

If she does, I'll just admit to it, if Lorna asks. Be honest.

Honesty was always the best policy. Even when it was painful. When Anna had discovered she had cancer early on in her pregnancy and the doctors had advised her to terminate, because her type of cancer was aggressive, they had taken some time to make their decision. Anna had wanted to continue with the pregnancy and, though he'd wanted to be the good guy and support her one hundred per cent in a decision about her own body and for their child, his honest opinion? Agreed with the doctors. And so he'd told her.

'I don't want you to die. Your cancer is aggressive, and if you wait to give birth who knows what will happen in those short months?'

'So what are you saying? I should terminate our child?'

'To give you the best chance of survival. We can always try for another child... We can't try for another you.'

She'd told him that by saying that he'd made her feel all alone. Abandoned almost, when he'd not wanted her to feel that way at all. But he'd been trying to do the best thing for her and this child was as much his as it was hers. He'd had to have his say, right? He was allowed an opinion.

And, of course, she'd continued with the pregnancy. He'd tried to marvel at every stage. The way her belly had grown. The first flutterings of movement. The feel of a first kick. Buying baby clothes in pink when they'd discovered it was a girl.

But as she'd grown, so had the cancer and though Anna had bloomed, he'd known something dark and insidious had also been growing within her and the doctors' decision to deliver her early had been a good one, even though

Anna had wanted to go to term to give her child the best chance of health and life. His decision to be honest about his feelings had caused an upset in their relationship, but he'd believed it vital to be honest. He'd always prided himself on it.

Surely he should be honest with Bella about his feelings, too? So that she was clear on how he felt? But what if she rejected his feelings, the way Anna had, to do her own thing?

Max headed into his own consultation room, closing the door behind him. Booting up his computer, settling into his chair, checking on results and letters that had come in overnight. He'd been given an admin hour first thing. His clinic didn't start until ten.

He saw that his patient Robert Heaney had been diagnosed with a DVT, as expected. That some bloods showed other patients were iron deficient and that another had pernicious anaemia. He called through to the reception manager, Saskia, and asked her to call the patient to arrange an appointment to discuss the results and come in for a B12 injection.

He lost himself in the paperwork, but couldn't help but think about Bella in the next room.

CHAPTER SIX

BELLA WAS JUST settling in, when there was a knock on her door.

Please don't be Max. Please don't be Max!

'Come in!' She forced a smile and relaxed her shoulders and beamed when she realised it was only Lorna. 'Hey. What's up?'

Lorna settled into a chair. 'Well, to be honest with you, that was going to be my question to you. Is everything all right?'

'Fine! Why?'

'I don't know, you just seemed a little…unsettled out there. Terse. Bad weekend?'

'No! Just a little…miscommunication, that's all. It's nothing. It's passed now.'

'Oh. Anything I can help with?'

'No. It's done. Honestly, everything is fine.'

'Weren't you and Max going to the funfair at the weekend? Did something happen between you two? The atmosphere was a little awkward out there and I only ask because, well, this is a small practice and, as the lead partner, I need to make sure that my doctors are all getting on okay.'

'I'm fine. Honestly. Like I say, it was just a miscommunication.'

'Between you and Max, or…?'

'We've settled it.'

'You're sure?'

'Yes.'

'You don't need a mediation, or anything?'

'No.' Bella smiled. 'It's not like we're married!' She laughed, imagining Max sliding a ring onto her finger. His eyes staring into hers. Stepping forward to seal their marriage with a kiss. 'It was something silly and I overreacted, that's all.'

'Okay. Well, I just want you to know that I'm here if you ever need to talk. I know I'm your boss and colleague, but I'd like to think that I'm here as your friend, too, so if at any time you want a chat…then I'm here. My door is always open, as they say.'

'Thanks, Lorna.'

She watched Lorna go, hoping that that would be the end of the matter. She didn't need her and Max's kiss to become a work issue, where Lorna got to weigh in. She'd only been in the job a couple of weeks and didn't want to cause trouble for anyone. Especially not this early. She wanted to put her roots down here. Raise Ewan in this peaceful and beautiful village.

I'm going to make a concerted effort to let Max know that everything is all right between us, because I can't have it going any other way.

Mr Colin Gatsby was her first patient of the day. Aged fifty-one, he came in with a smile and ruddy cheeks.

'Hello, I'm Dr Nightingale. How can I help you today?'

'It's this redness on my face, Doctor. Itching like crazy, it is, and I can't stop scratching at it.'

It did look quite sore and red. 'And how long has it been like this?'

'Three days. I thought maybe it was too much sun, but I've never had anything like this before. The occasional blotch on a cheek, when I've been stressed or something, but it's never itched like this. I couldn't enjoy the fair yesterday, because all I wanted to do was scratch.'

'Okay, is it just on your face, or anywhere else?'

'Just my face. Mainly my cheeks. It goes up to my temples and a little down my neck. I put some aloe vera on it, but it just burned every time.'

'Is it all right if I examine you?'

He nodded.

Bella washed her hands and then put on some gloves and examined Colin's face. The skin was extremely dry and rough. 'What's your cleaning routine?'

'Soap and water. Always has been.'

'You shouldn't be using soap. Not with your skin, it's very dry. You've got something called rosacea. It's common and it can come and go, but certain things can trigger it. Sunlight, heat, exercise, hot drinks, spicy food… We need to change your skin routine.'

'Skin routine? I'm not sure I've ever had one!'

'Well, we need to change that, Mr Gatsby, if you want the itching to stop and to keep control of this.'

'Like what?'

'Well, your skin is very dry and so we need you to start using a moisturiser, every day. Preferably twice a day, morning and night, before bed.'

'Like what the wife uses?'

'You can, but I could also prescribe a specific one that's for sensitive skin, that doesn't contain any perfumes or unnecessary ingredients that might antagonise your skin.'

'All right. Is that all I have to do?'

'No. I'm going to prescribe some metronidazole gel. It's an antibiotic gel that you apply to the reddened area each day, after you've washed and moisturised, and then, after that, I want you to use a suncream, every day. Nothing less than factor fifty. Every time you go out. Whether it's sunny and hot, or the middle of winter and foggy. *Every time* you go out.'

'Really?'

'Yes. Wait for the gel to dry properly, before you use the suncream.'

'That sounds like an awful lot to do, Doc.'

'It won't take you a minute or so more than your ordinary wash in the morning, but it's important, Mr Gatsby. Believe you me, if you lived in Spain or another hot country with your skin, it would look and feel a lot worse. The UV light aggravates rosacea.'

'Oh, I didn't know that. And with all these creams and potions, it should get better, should it?'

'Yes. You can use the metronidazole gel for a few months, but, after that, moisturising and protecting your skin with suncream every day should help a great deal and if it comes back or gets worse, you come and see me again.'

'Right. Okay. Well, thanks.'

'No problem at all. I've sent a script for those items to your usual chemist.'

'Lovely. All right, thanks, Doc. And thanks for seeing me.'

'It was a pleasure to meet you.'

She wished she could get rid of her own blushing every time she interacted with Max. Imagine how much easier life would be if she could just apply a cream that would stop him from being able to see how interested she was in him. How he made her feel.

It would certainly have made yesterday easier to bear.

Max was just finishing for lunch, when there was a knock at his door. When it opened, he was surprised to see Bella standing there with a tray. Two mugs of tea, two red velvet cupcakes and their lunchboxes from the fridge. 'Care to accept an olive branch?' she asked, smiling, her face full of hope.

How could he say no? And he was delighted that she had come to him and made this move. 'Gladly! Come on in!'

She smiled. 'I thought I'd take a leaf out of Oliver's book. He always takes Lorna a cup of tea in the morning and so I stole the idea and thought I'd bring you lunch, tea and dessert.' She placed the tray on his table.

'This looks great! But it's such a lovely day outside. What do you say we pack this up and go sit on the green? There's a bench under that big horse-chestnut tree, so there'll be shade.'

She glanced out of the window. 'Sounds like a plan.'

They transferred the tea into two travel mugs, wrapped the cupcakes and carried their lunches outside to the green. As expected in the middle of the day, it was popular and there were a couple of other people spread out on a blanket in the shade, reading books.

He also thought that Bella might feel a little more comfortable out here in public. Though he greatly appreciated her action to bring his lunch to his room, where they would have been in private, he saw no reason as to why they couldn't still have a private conversation out in public. And this way, they got to enjoy the warm, sunny day and the fresh air, after being cooped up in their consulting rooms. Made everything a little less intense.

'This is wonderful,' she said, sitting down on the bench.

'Perfect spot,' he agreed. Was now the time to try and apologise?

'Lorna spoke to me earlier today.'

'Oh?'

'Asked if there was a problem between us.' She gave him a quick glance. Smiled. Looked away and bit into her sandwich. When she'd finished chewing, she said, 'I told her it was settled.'

'Okay. I mean, it is, right? I'd hate to think that what I did yesterday would ruin anything here. This is an amazing place, with amazing people, and I want to settle here and feel good here and I'd never forgive myself if I'd screwed that up for you.'

She looked at him. 'You didn't screw it up.'

'I am sorry about what happened.'

Her cheeks coloured. 'It was just a kiss, right?'

He nodded. 'Right.' He could certainly view it that way, even if he didn't want to. That kiss had meant something for him. He'd never kissed another woman since Anna and yet he'd felt able to kiss Bella. Had wanted to kiss Bella. Over and over again. She stirred feelings within him. Feelings that he couldn't contain, but tried to.

'Something spontaneous. Unplanned. And I could have stopped it, too. I also hold responsibility here, and for that? I apologise.'

She was right. She could have stopped it, could have pushed him away, only she hadn't.

She'd kissed him back!

Why hadn't he thought about that? He'd been so busy blaming himself, he'd not thought too much about her response to the kiss. But then again, he was good at blaming himself. He blamed himself for getting Anna pregnant. If she'd not been pregnant, then she would have fought her cancer before it spread and she might not have died. He blamed himself for not fighting harder for a termination. He blamed himself for not enjoying her pregnancy and feeling anger towards an innocent baby. And he blamed himself that his wonderful daughter didn't have a mother.

He was good at laying the blame for everything at his own doorstep. Maybe he ought to try not to do that any more. Maybe with Bella, life could be different. She was certainly making him see things from another viewpoint.

Somehow, he felt a little lighter.

Max smiled his thanks for her apology, even though he felt as though she didn't have to make it.

'You know, in the spirit of goodwill and friendship and getting us both back on an even keel, I had an interesting email arrive in my inbox today.'

'Oh?' He was all for getting them back on an even keel. He'd not liked how it had felt for them not to be getting along. It had felt at odds with his contentment and happiness.

'I'm on the mailing list for the Todmore Maltings in the next village. It used to be an old Victorian factory building, but now it's a set of artists' studios, alongside a pottery, a gallery and a café. But every month, they do public events and things and I noticed in the email today that they're holding a pottery experience for beginners next Friday afternoon.'

'You should do it! You told me you always fancied doing pottery.'

She nodded, smiling. 'And you did, too. We both have an early finish next Friday and it just seems meant to be, so, as friends, would you like to go with me? I'll happily go on my own, but it's nice to have someone there that you know.'

Bella really was offering him the olive branch. She'd meant it when she came to his consulting room.

Well, if she could put all that upset behind her, then so could he! 'Er, sure. Would we be back in time to pick up the kids from school?'

'Easily. Want me to forward you the email, so you can see the details of it?'

'That would be great.'

'I just thought it might be a fun thing to do and…well, I can't think of anyone else who would like to go with me.'

'Ah. A pity invite.' He laughed.

'A hundred per cent!' She laughed, too. 'No, seriously, just…de-escalating a situation is all.'

'Well, as long as you can restrain yourself, you know.'

She gave him a playful shove and he laughed.

This was better. This was much better. He almost felt as if they were back to normal, as long as he didn't allow his mind to go off on flights of fancy of the two of them shaping bowls on the same pottery wheel, as it was in that film. What was it called?

Max couldn't remember and that part didn't

really matter. What mattered was that everything was fine between them again.

Just as it was meant to be.

Bella was glad that they'd talked. That the white flag of truce had been shown, the olive branch accepted and now they were back to normal.

She'd debated mentioning the pottery experience, but she remembered he'd mentioned wanting to give it a try and how else could she prove to him that she wanted to put the kiss behind them and just move on?

By showing I was happy to spend some time with him.

And unlike in the pod, they would not be alone. They would be in a class, with other people, out in public. It would be fine. No accidental kisses. No forced proximity. No opportunity to stare into each other's eyes and forget the world.

It would be fun. Light-hearted. A laugh. Maybe they'd both get to make something they'd be proud of. And once it was done, they would have moved past the awkwardness of the weekend and how it had felt to walk to school with him this morning.

Eva Watts was her first patient of the afternoon. She came in looking pale, with dark circles under her eyes. 'I'm just so tired all the time. It's like I've got no energy to do anything.'

'How long have you felt this way?'

'A couple of months, to be honest. I kept thinking it would get better, but it just seems to be getting worse. I'm having headaches, too, and I've got this weird tingling in my fingers.'

Bella examined her, noting her pallor, her low blood pressure and the fact that Eva seemed a little underweight for her height. And she had bruising on her forearms that looked as though she'd been held down. It was worrying. 'How's your appetite?'

'Not great, to be honest.'

'Do you eat red meat? Leafy greens?'

'No. Chicken and fish usually, with rice or pasta, that kind of thing. My boyfriend is on this health kick. He goes to the gym, he's training to be a bodybuilder and he didn't want to be tempted by bad things in the house, so we eat a very simple diet.'

The boyfriend sounded as if he might be much stronger than her, then. 'Does he take supplements?'

'There's a cupboard full.'

'Do you take any?'

She shook her head. 'I'm not training and he doesn't like muscly women.'

'What are your periods like?'

She sighed. 'Heavy. Painful. Like clots. I flood a lot.'

Bella nodded. 'I think you might be anaemic, Eva. I'd like to do a blood test to confirm.'

'Oh. Okay.'

'We'll do it now, if that's all right?'

Eva nodded.

Bella opened her cupboard, where she kept her blood-test equipment, but she was all out of purple vials and needed to go to the stockroom to get some more. 'I won't be a moment.' She excused herself and headed to the room where they kept everything a surgery could need— blood-sampling equipment, the emergency bag with defibrillator, oxygen canisters, swabs, pads, bandages, saline, tongue depressors, tools used for IUD insertions, scissors, tweezers, everything and anything was kept in there in neatly labelled drawers and maintained by their health care assistant, Carrie, who ordered the stock.

The purple vials were on the back wall, with all the other colours. She was getting a very bad feeling about Eva and her boyfriend. Those bruises looked painful and as if fingers had been squeezed tightly about her wrists. As she reached for a tray of tubes, the door behind her opened.

'Oh! Hi.'

Max.

She turned and smiled. 'Hi! What have you run out of?'

He laughed, nervously. 'Oh! Um…plasters,

of all things. Paper cut.' He held up his finger, which was bleeding.

She knew where the plasters were and she was closest to them. She pulled open the drawer. 'How did you do that?'

'Refilling the printer with blood forms.'

'Ouch. Been there. You'll need an antiseptic wipe, too, hold on.' The box of wipes was in the same drawer as the plasters and she pulled one out and ripped open the packet and took hold of his hand without thinking about it. In doctor mode. Fixer mode.

Not until she was holding his hand and wiping away the blood did she think about where they were and what they were doing. In a store cupboard. Alone. Up close. Holding his hand!

Bella swallowed hard and tried not to blush, focusing intently on cleaning his wound, which was just over a centimetre in length. He'd really sliced himself well. It occurred to her that maybe she ought to have put gloves on, but it was too late now, and she just figured she'd wash her hands really well when she got back to her room, where her patient was waiting.

My patient!

'I...er...' She backed away and handed him the plaster, blushing furiously. 'You can do this part. I have a patient waiting, sorry.'

And she rushed past him, pulling open the

stockroom door and leaving as quickly as she could. She blew out her cheeks and felt the coolness of the air in the corridor.

Wow. That was close.

Not that anything had been going to happen. More that they had been in forced proximity again, so quickly after the kiss, and it had simply reminded her—her body being an absolute traitor!—that another kiss would be a wonderful thing.

Bella apologised to Eva when she got back to the room and washed her hands. 'Now, about your heavy periods you mentioned…did you want to try something to help with those?'

'Like what?'

'Well, it's been shown that going on the contraceptive pill can help lighten periods, though obviously not everyone wants to take hormones.'

'That might be helpful, actually. My boyfriend, he doesn't like wearing condoms and I don't want to get pregnant, so…'

'Is there any chance you could be pregnant now?'

Eva shrugged. 'Maybe.'

'Okay. I'll add hCG testing to the blood test as well just to confirm.' She put on gloves and took her patient's sample. 'We should have the results for this back in one or two days, but in the meantime I'm going to prescribe you some iron tablets to take, just to be on the safe side. It's best to take them with food and if you can swallow them with orange juice then that helps with the absorption. If you are pregnant, then it's totally fine to take.'

'Do I have to call to get the results?'

'We'll text you with the results.' She checked that they had the correct mobile number, which they did. 'If the pregnancy test is positive, then I'll call to talk to you. I take it it's safe to call you on that number?'

'Why wouldn't it be?'

'I couldn't help but notice your bruising, Eva.'

Eva instantly looked down and pulled down her sleeves. 'It's nothing. I ran into a door.'

'I understand, but…a door doesn't make bruises like that. Fingertips do. Hands do. Does your boyfriend have any…anger issues?'

Eva looked down at the ground, utterly defeated. 'He doesn't mean it,' she said quietly. 'I get things wrong and he gets upset.'

'If you're in danger, Eva, I can help you.'

'I'm not.'

'I can put you in touch with people who can help.'

'I'm fine. Can I go now? He's waiting for me outside.'

Bella didn't want to let her go, but what could she do? She had no idea how bad things were, or if this was an isolated incident. 'All right. But I want to see you again in a week's time. You can tell him it's to discuss your results, but I'd like to check on you and, if you're willing to consent, I'd like to disclose details of this consultation with my designated adult safeguarding lead.'

'Why?'

'Because I have an ethical duty of care to you and you've told me that your partner mishandles his anger and I've seen evidence of bruising on your arms, which will go onto your legal medical record, detailing my concerns.'

'What will this other person do?'

'They'll read my report. They may get in touch with you to talk further about your needs and your safety.'

Eva looked uncomfortable, but curious. 'But who is it?'

'It's Dr Lorna Hudson.'

'I know her. She's nice.'

Bella smiled. 'She's very nice and is extremely good at what she does.'

'What if…what if Ben finds out?'

'We would do our absolute utmost to ensure that only you are spoken to about this in a safe way that would not endanger you to any further harm.'

She nodded.

'You're giving me consent? To talk to Lorna? To see what help we can give you?'

She nodded again. 'I'm so tired.'

Bella reached forward and placed her hand on Eva's. 'I understand. But we know now and we can help you. Let me make an appointment for you. Same time, next week?'

'That'll be fine. He's away next week on a training camp.'

'Perfect.'

Eva Watts' blood-test results came back showing that, yes, she was very anaemic, so Bella was glad that she'd already got her on iron tablets. The medication should help her feel better and hopefully give her more energy, by correcting the imbalance in her system. Thankfully, she wasn't pregnant, either.

She spoke to Lorna and informed her of her safeguarding concerns for her patient.

In the meantime, Bella tried to continue as normal. Working with Max. Walking to school with him each day. He was so easy to talk to when they kept their conversations light-hearted and they both intensely avoided talking about the funfair kiss.

The kids were getting on great at school and party invites and sleepover invites were starting to come in from other kids, as their friendship group expanded.

She was beginning to feel settled in Clearbrook and was happy. As Friday rolled around and she and Max could go to Todmore for the pottery class, she was excited and nervous. Max offered to drive and it took them about twenty minutes to drive there. When they got to Todmore Maltings, they were given directions to their class and found a room filled with a variety of people, old and young alike. Their instructor was a middle-aged woman called Celia and she told them that today they would construct a decorated tile, using a technique called slip and score. Slip and score allowed for joining two pieces of clay together. The potter would scratch marks on the surfaces to be joined and then a liquid mixture of clay and water would be applied to join them together.

Celia showed them a variety of tiles made by previous students to give them an idea of what they could achieve and set them to work, with paper and pencils first, so they could draw their designs.

Bella decided to make a tile with fruit on it. An apple. A banana. Cherries. Max was bolder. He wanted a cat and a mouse. Once they'd drawn out their pieces, they were left to try and shape the clay and discovered it was a lot harder than it looked. Their first attempts looked like something a child had tried to create and they couldn't help but laugh at each other's attempts. It was kind of freeing to play with clay and it was almost like being back at school, but eventually they got there and attached their pieces of shaped clay to the tile.

Not bad for first-timers, she thought, glancing at Max, noticing that he had a smudge of clay on his face, just above his beard line. 'You've got something here,' she said, pointing at her own face for comparison.

'Oh, thanks.' Max tried to wipe at the mark but it wasn't coming off.

'Here. Let me.' She grabbed a clean cloth, dipped it in water and then leaned towards him to help wipe away the clay. One hand on his jaw to position his face so she could see what she was doing. It felt weirdly exciting to be staring at him so intently like this. Touching his face. Wiping at the clay smudge. So close to his mouth.

His lips. She knew how his mouth had felt upon her own. The heat of their kiss. How it had made her feel. Awakening her body for the first time in a long time, and now that Max had woken the beast? It wanted feeding.

Part of her more sensible, logical mind told her to be more forceful, to get it done quickly, to not drag this out, but that voice got drowned out.

Bella took her time. Dabbing gently. Not wanting to give him a red mark. Wanting to be gentle. Softly wiping his face, trying to focus on the clay mark, rather than the fact that she knew he was staring at her face, his lips parted, breathing hesitantly.

She was fascinated by the way his beard grew. Looking at every bristle. At the tones of his skin, the way his cheekbone shaped his face. Her fingertips on his jaw held him gently, but she wondered how fast his pulse would be going if she could press the flats of her fingertips to his neck. Very fast, no doubt. As her own was.

The clay was coming off. It had dried upon his face, so had been difficult to begin with, but now it was coming off more easily and she realised, very quickly, that she didn't want this moment to end, but end it had to. 'There you go. All done.' She managed a smile, but her insides were in turmoil. Her blood felt hot. As if it were fizzing with sparks of electricity, and she was so aware of him.

'Thanks.' His voice sounded gruff and he had to clear his throat and say it again.

Celia told them the work would go into the drying room and they could come back for next week's class, where they could be painted and then fired.

Bella and Max were working the next week,

so Celia told them they could take their pieces home as they were.

'Shaping clay was harder than I thought. I would have liked to have had a go on a potter's wheel, though,' Bella said, laughing nervously.

'You can never have enough wonky bowls in the house,' he mused.

'Absolutely.' She smiled at him in amused agreement. She could remember as a child making an ashtray out of clay for her dad once, at school. It had been the ugliest thing ever, but her father had treasured it and used it as a place to drop his house keys every time he came in from work. Maybe one day, Ewan would make something for her and she would treasure it.

Travelling back to Clearbrook, she was very aware of Max in the seat next to her. The way his hands held the steering wheel. How, on occasion, when he changed gear, his hand came close to her thigh, and she found herself imagining how it might feel to have Max's hands trace up her thighs. How it would feel to have him stroke that soft, sensitive skin on her inner thigh...

It made her heart pound and she couldn't believe she was having such thoughts. When she'd first seen him at the school, he'd looked like the exact kind of guy that would be dangerous to her. Of course, she hadn't really known him then and, since then, they'd become very close—

working with one another, living near one another, spending time in each other's houses...
The situation had changed and she thought that maybe, just maybe, he might be different.

Why? She wasn't sure. But she knew she was incredibly attracted to him and since the kiss, there had been moments—in the store cupboard, at the pottery class, in the car—when she'd found herself wishing that she weren't so afraid. Weren't so wary. So that she could allow herself to indulge. Perhaps in just the physical? Keep emotions out of it, but allow herself to sate her lust, because what would be wrong in that? People did it all the time.

But not people who work closely together.
Not people who are neighbours.
Not people who ought to know better.
Then who?

As they waited for Ewan and Rosie to grab their coats at pickup time, they were given paintings that the kids had completed that day. Ewan had painted a rocket going up into space and Rosie had painted a garden full of flowers.

'Those are amazing, guys,' Max said, admiring them both.

'What's for dinner? I'm starving!' Ewan asked.

It was Max's turn to host. 'Fajitas. Is that okay?'

'Yum!'

Bella was beginning to feel that everything was becoming complicated with Max again after that little blip at the funfair. She'd tried being in his company, pretending that everything was fine, and she'd almost made herself believe it, but was it really? She'd sat next to him at pottery today and they'd been laughing and enjoying each other's company and, yes, he'd given her all the warm, wonderful feelings, but that was okay, because, she'd told herself, nothing was going to happen.

And then she'd helped to clean his face. Had glanced once into his eyes and seen something reflected back that had told her that even he was struggling to pretend that nothing had happened between them. She'd seen wonder and want in his eyes, too. He was handsome. Sexy. But neither of them could dare to overstep the mark. She could still appreciate his beauty. Could still steal glances at him when he wasn't looking. Could wonder as to why he was still single. A guy like him...should have been snapped up by now, surely?

He was a dedicated father. A professional. Gorgeous. Clever. Kind. Why hadn't he sought out another relationship? Had he really been alone since his wife died? It almost didn't seem possible. She was curious about him and her curiosity didn't seem to want to fade. She needed to know more about him and what he wanted from the future. A headache was beginning to form. Tension? Stress? From all the frowning as she tried to work him out?

As they stood in the kitchen together, she chopping up salad, he warming the tortilla wraps in the oven, she found herself asking him exactly that. 'Do you think you'll ever settle down again? Like, get married, again?'

He turned to look at her. 'Why are you asking that?'

'I don't know. It's just that, you know, clearly you have a lot to offer someone. I just wondered why you'd not pursued settling down again. Or have you?'

Max let out a heavy sigh. 'I don't know. I always told myself I could never, but, as Rosie gets older, I have thought about what it might be like to be with someone again. I haven't before because, well, it was just too soon. Everything I've been through makes you wary of wanting to get close to someone else again. I mean, imagine if they got sick? I'd panic straight away.'

'So you're looking for someone who has one hundred per cent of their health?' She smiled.

He laughed. 'Yes. And someone who loves Rosie as much as I do. Someone who doesn't mind my long hours.' He shook his head. 'Basically, I'm looking for the impossible. How about you? You ever considered it?'

'Wow. Um… I hadn't. Being betrayed like that, abandoned like that, with no support for his own child, I… It kind of interfered with the way that I view guys. I mean, honestly? I do not know a single guy that has never let down a woman. My dad let down my mother. My brothers haven't always stayed true to their partners. I had Blake, who cheated on me. Friends whose marriages have broken down because of cheating, too. I just… I'd need a guy who couldn't ever possibly let me down.'

He smiled at her. 'Are you looking for the impossible, too?'

'Maybe. Is that so wrong, though? To want to protect yourself from future hurt?'

'No. It isn't. I get it. We're all vulnerable, but I guess, if we both want to be with someone in the future, we're just going to have to have faith and place our trust in them.'

'How do you do that, exactly? When you've been as hurt as I have? As you have?'

Max shook his head. 'I don't know. But if you find out, promise you'll let me know.'

She smiled, sadly. 'I promise.' The conversation had got serious. Asking him about whether he'd get into another serious relationship. Was she curious in general, or for herself? Could she see herself with Max and Rosie? As a blended family?

It was a weighty topic and worthy of further consideration, but Bella honestly didn't know where to go from here. Say something more? Make a joke to break the tension?

Luckily, Max came to the rescue. 'Okay! The fajitas are done. Want to call the kids in?'

She was grateful to him for changing the subject. 'Sure.'

Max had struggled to get that conversation out of his head all weekend. He was only willing to settle down with someone who technically couldn't possibly exist. How could he guarantee that the person he chose would be free of any health concerns, now or in the future?

He couldn't.

That wasn't how humans worked. They were made up of many moving parts. Filled with trillions of cells, fuelled by hormones and blood, and anything could go wrong with any singular part at any time in their lives.

So, was he doomed to failure? Doomed to be alone? Not willing to risk his heart in case someone got sick?

And Bella. She was looking for someone who wouldn't let her down. Wouldn't cheat on her. He would like to think that person existed. He

would like to think that he was the type of guy
that wouldn't let her down, but was it possible?
Human beings were fallible. They made mistakes. They made sacrifices, they told white lies
in the hopes of protecting someone. Sometimes
bigger lies, to protect themselves. He wasn't a
cheat and never could be. It went against all he
held dear, but would he disappoint her in other
ways? Upset her? Break her heart by directly
opposing her own wishes?

They were being honest with each other now,
but what about later on? And the reason he kept
thinking about whether he could be with Bella
was what he'd felt during that kiss. And again in
the stockroom when she'd tended his cut. In the
pottery class when she'd cleaned his face of clay.

Those moments, short as they were, had been
so intense and all he'd been able to do, in that
pottery class as she'd dabbed at his face with a
cloth, was to think of that kiss. To look into her
face and see her eyes so dark with concentration
and secrets that he'd wanted the world to stop,
so that he could find out what they were. What
she was thinking, because he could see that she
was just as discombobulated as he was!

Every spare moment, he spent thinking about
Bella. About how well the two of them got on,
about how good the two of them might be together. The kids got along, they were the best

of friends. He and Bella were clearly attracted to one another. Surely they could be something amazing? If they were both brave enough to take the risk?

Were they brave enough? Could he be that brave so that he could have Bella? Could she be that brave to have him? To risk it all on the possibility of happiness? Was possibility enough?

His first patient of the day was Mary Connor, who'd come to see him after receiving her results from her scan at the neurologist.

She sat in front of him, holding the letter. 'It says it's corti…cortico…' She sighed and struggled with the pronunciation.

'Corticobasal degeneration.'

'I'm not sure I fully understand what that is. I did speak to him briefly at a consultation when he gave me the results, but I was just so overwhelmed and I'm not sure I took anything in. Can you tell me just exactly what this is?'

'Sure. It's a condition that is a type of dementia and it's something we can manage, but not cure.'

'Dementia, yes. I got that. So I'm going to lose my memory, then?'

'It's more than that, I'm afraid. This condition is caused by the body failing to break down a particular protein called tau. When tau builds up in the brain, it forms these clumps that can be quite obstructive and it leads to a person being unable to move well, speak or swallow, as well as affecting memory.'

'Oh, my goodness...'

'You remember you came because of problems with your arm and you mentioned your memory issues. These are early symptoms you've been having and it's good that it's been caught early, because we can give you preventative medicine.'

'The doc gave me pregabalin.'

'Yes. It should help with any pains you feel.'

'But that's all? Just pain? It won't stop anything else?'

'I'm afraid that we don't have much to prevent this disease, but we can treat the more symptomatic issues.'

'But I'm going to most likely end up in a wheelchair? Or in a bed? Unable to think? Or speak? Or swallow?' Mary's eyes welled up.

Max passed her the tissues and she took one, blowing her nose.

'We can't be sure how the disease will progress in individuals and not everyone gets all the same symptoms. We will meet up regularly though and monitor you and do what we can, as and when the need to step in is required. I can also put you in touch with support groups and talking therapies, if you or your husband need it.'

'I just never thought a little tremor would succeed in telling me my life could soon be over. There's so much I still wanted to do.'

'And there's no reason why you shouldn't still do them.'

She nodded and dabbed at her eyes. 'You never think it's going to end like this, huh? You think you'll live for ever and then, maybe when you're in your eighties or nineties, you'll go to sleep one night and just never wake up. Go peacefully. That's what I always wanted. But it turns out in this life you don't get what you expect.'

'I guess not.' He felt bad. He felt that he ought to be comforting her in many more ways, but right now, whilst she was upset, he felt as if his words might be empty.

'I guess I could make arrangements for that clinic. The one that helps people pass in the way that they choose. Peaceably and in control, whilst they still have it.'

He didn't know what to say. His calling to be a doctor was to help people and to prevent suffering. But he was subject to laws and guidelines.

'And this isn't fair on my husband! What he'll have to watch me go through, because this, my illness, it doesn't just affect me, does it? It affects him, too.'

He understood her anger and her frustration. He'd always thought he would be married to Anna his entire life. That they would share memories. Make memories. Travel. Raise a family. Have grandchildren and great-grandchildren and, as Mary suggested, live into their golden years together and fall asleep holding hands.

But life hadn't given him or Anna that. Life had taken Anna from him, cruelly. And much too soon. At the end she'd slipped away quietly in her sleep. But not before he'd seen her moaning in pain. Not before he'd seen her crying about leaving Rosie. Had endured long hours at her bedside holding her hand with her unaware because the morphine had knocked her out so well. He'd listened to those last breaths and then the silence that had followed and there'd been nothing easy about that. Not for either of them.

He didn't want to go through that with anyone ever again and he felt for Mary that she possibly faced such an ending, too.

What was the lesson from that? To take happiness whenever he could get it? To treasure every moment and stop second-guessing himself? Why was he torturing himself over Bella? They could be happy, couldn't they? They just had to try. Better to have loved and lost than never to have loved at all.

At morning break, he stepped outside to grab some fresh air and found Bella standing outside, too. She hadn't seen him, but she stood over in the small practice garden, her back to him, one hand up against her head.

'Hey.'

She turned, looking pale, with dark shadows under her eyes.

Instantly, he was alarmed. 'Are you all right?'

'Just a headache. I've taken some paracetamol, but this one's not shifting. Probably because I didn't get much sleep last night—I'm just tired.' She smiled a soothing, dreamy smile.

'Have you been drinking enough water? Most headaches are caused by dehydration.'

'I know. I read that study too and, yes, I have, I just needed some fresh air.'

He felt reassured. 'It is beautiful out here, isn't it?'

The garden was small and private and had a wooden bench dedicated to a doctor long gone. *Dr Bartleby. Who loved this garden.*

There was a cherry tree. Hollyhocks that stood tall and proud, brandishing their dark, scarlet blooms, foxgloves in lilac that were feeding the bees. Dwarf sunflowers and lupins and chrysanthemums. A small rockery with heathers and a tiny water feature, so that they could hear the soothing sound of babbling water, even though they were nowhere near the brook that ran through the village.

'It is. I'm so grateful we have this space at work.'

He stared at her for a moment. 'Can I ask you a question?'

She turned to him, smiled. 'Of course.'

'We all get trained on how to deliver bad news to a patient. How to be professional. How to maintain that emotional distance, so that you can be clear, but also friendly and approachable, but they never teach you how to deal with afterwards. For the medic, I mean. I had to explain to a patient today that she isn't most likely going to die in the way that she would like, but instead in a much more difficult and distressing way, and sometimes, I just...' He sighed. 'I can't reconcile that in my mind. She's such a sweet lady and she doesn't deserve what's going to happen to her!'

'Does anybody? I'm sorry you've had to do that.'

'Every time I do, I remember what it was like to sit in that room at the hospital and be told by doctors that Anna's cancer was terminal. I know what it's like to be the one in the chair. I know what it's like to have your world, your future, turned upside down and I just wonder how that doctor felt when they left us, afterwards. Left us sitting in that room, holding our newborn daughter. Did they get upset? Did they have to take a break? Or did they just go right into the next room and deliver much happier news to someone else?'

She took a step towards him. 'This world will always be filled with unanswered questions. We won't ever get the answers we truly seek and maybe that's the whole point? Isn't life supposed to be a mystery and an enigma and we all just do our best to bumble our way through it and hope that we don't get hurt too much in the process?'

'And what if you have been hurt?' he asked, his voice low and soft. 'How do you get brave enough to try again?'

She looked deeply into his eyes. Standing close now. 'I guess you try and find ways to heal yourself. The best you can.'

He stared back. She had such beautiful eyes. Soft and alluring. A deep blue. Her skin looking so perfectly pale and creamy in the sunlight that shone down into the garden. The sun highlighting her cheekbones. Causing a perfect shadow just beneath her full lower lip.

He couldn't help himself. He reached up to rub his thumb over it and her lips parted. Max wanted to kiss her so badly, but he remembered what had happened the last time that he'd just followed his impulses and he didn't like how it had gone.

But something surprising happened instead.

Bella stepped *towards* him. She laid a hand

upon *his* chest. She paused briefly, her eyes glazed with desire, and suddenly her lips were upon his and she was kissing him and the world turned upside down and inside out as he kissed her back, pulling her into his arms and allowing the kiss to become deeper. More intense.

The same thing happened as before. The world went silent and stopped. The noise from cars in the distance disappeared. The sound of bumblebees silenced. The aroma from the lavender fields was no longer there. It was just the two of them, standing in a void, bodies pressed up against one another, and Bella felt wonderful in his arms. Her softness, her curves. The way she tasted, the way she made him feel.

Alive again! After so long of living in a strange half-existence that he'd once thought was fine.

This was what had been missing from his life. This connection that you could only feel with another person who cared for you as much as you cared for them. This meeting of spirits. This coming together, and all from the power of a simple kiss.

When it ended, the world returned and part of him hesitated, unsure of what to say, wondering if she would panic again and blank him, or act embarrassed, or say it was a mistake.

Please don't say that, Bella! I couldn't bear to

hear you say that what I just experienced with you was a mistake.

She looked up at him nervously, then a smile crept across her face. She blushed.

And he smiled, too. Maybe everything would be all right, after all? 'Are you okay?'

'Yes. Are you?'

'Yes. I'm feeling…apprehensive. I don't know what this means, but I know I don't want to mess this up.'

She sucked in a deep breath and nodded. 'Nor me.'

'So, how do we proceed? I mean…how do you want this to go? We both have so much at stake here. It's complicated.'

'It is. I guess we…take it slow. We don't rush things. Or miss steps. We go slow and carefully.'

'Yes.' He wanted to kiss her again. But there were patients waiting and they had a job to do. 'We should get back to work for now.'

She nodded.

'You're definitely okay?'

A smile. 'Yes.'

She'd been hesitant to kiss him, but had been compelled to, unable to stop herself, ignoring the fierce headache that still raged in her skull, making her feel nauseous. *Damn these migraines I keep having.*

The pain in her head had almost ruined the perfection of that kiss.

This second kiss had been everything she had imagined it would be like, after her experience at the funfair. She'd held back from kissing him so many times since that day and she'd been proud of her self-control, despite her physical and emotional attraction to Max. But today? She just hadn't been able to hold back. He'd looked and sounded so beat. That appointment that he'd had had really upset him. It might surprise the general public to realise that GPs were not automatons that sat in a room with patients for ten minutes, listened to their symptoms, gave them a prescription and sent them on their merry way.

GPs were human, too. And they felt patients' pain and they empathised with them sometimes, on levels the public could never know. Because they had to be professional, but sometimes, when patients left the room and the GP was alone again...

It could hurt.

Perhaps because that patient's situation mirrored an experience the doctor had faced, or one of their family members had faced, either in the past, or much more recently.

Clearly, Max had had one of those today and she'd wanted to make him feel better, yes, but she'd also wanted to let him know that she was there for him.

She liked him very much. Rosie, too. But that didn't make any of this less scary. Would he come to disappoint her as all other guys had? Would he ever walk away and leave her because she wasn't enough?

Back in her room, she took more paracetamol, glad that her neurology appointment was soon so they could rule some conditions out. Bella was sure it was just tension headaches. Stress headaches. Migraines. Her father had always had bad heads, she'd probably just taken after him. And doctors made the worst patients anyway, because they knew all the horrors and were brilliant at leaping to conclusions. 'If it looks like a horse and it sounds like a horse, then think horse, not zebras.' That was what her mum had always said and it was true.

It had to be migraines. All the symptoms were there and she'd been under a lot of stress, lately. Her blood pressure had shown that. A house-move. A new job. Making sure that Ewan was settled and happy. Her tensions with Max. She'd been putting herself on the back burner a little too much.

All I need to do now is be happy and enjoy my life.

CHAPTER SEVEN

IN THE SPIRIT of taking care of herself, that weekend, whilst Ewan was watching cartoons inside, Bella took a chair into her small back garden, along with a sketchpad and a pencil, and began to draw the flowers that she could see.

There was a beautiful calla lily that had flowered, its white bloom reaching for the sky, having launched from a plethora of long green leaves. At its heart was a long yellow spadix, powdered with pollen, awaiting a bee.

It was a beautiful, graceful plant and she could feel herself relaxing as she drew it, long, free strokes of the pencil filling the page to capture the plant's elegance.

'You know that's highly poisonous, right?'

She turned at Max's voice, surprise crossing her face. 'How did you get out here?'

'Ewan let me in.'

'What? I've told him to not answer the door without my permission.' She knew she would have to have words with him later on. It was fine this time—after all, her guest was Max. 'But what if you'd been someone else? Someone dangerous?'

Max raised an eyebrow. 'In Clearbrook?'

'You never know. Do you let Rosie open the door without checking?'

Max smiled. 'Touché.'

She got up out of her chair and peered behind him. 'Where's Rosie?'

'Watching the cartoons with Ewan.'

'Oh.' She smiled at him and stepped towards him, pulling him to one side, away from the gaze of the windows and back door, and sneaked a kiss from him. 'Hi.'

'Hi.'

'Is it really poisonous?' She lifted up her pad and gazed at her drawing of the lily.

'It surely is. I did a shift in an A & E once—triaging minors—some kid came in with his parents. His mouth was all red and looked burned and raw. It was swollen and he had some difficulty breathing and he also kept being sick.'

'Poor kid!'

'We weren't sure what it was. We figured that maybe he'd ingested something, but even the parents were clueless. Said he'd been out playing in the garden. The dad had recently filmed a video in their back garden and showed us, so we could see what was there, and he had calla lilies. The kid had eaten one as a bet with his brother.'

'I don't think Ewan would do that, but maybe I should get rid of that one.' She turned to look at the plant that just a moment ago she'd thought was graceful and beautiful, eyeing it with distaste now and concern. 'Was the kid okay?'

Max nodded. 'He'd not eaten too much before he realised he was in trouble. The calla lily contains calcium oxalate crystals that feel like microscopic needles. Thankfully the crystals don't break down in the human body, so he couldn't suffer from whole body poisoning. He'd not eaten enough for that to happen. We gave him cooling things—milk, yoghurt and prescribed his parents to allow him to have lots of ice lollies to soothe his throat of damage—but we kept him in for a little while to observe his breathing. Then he went home.'

'Scary.' She looked him up and down, admiring him. 'Did you need something?'

'I did, yes.'

'What was it?'

He smiled. 'To see you.'

Bella chuckled. 'Oh. I see. Well...mission accomplished.'

He leaned in for another kiss, after checking they weren't being observed. The press of his lips upon hers caused her heart to race and her temperature to rise.

'Actually, there was something,' he said.

She looked up at him, smiling.

'I wondered if you'd like to go out for a meal with me one evening.'

'A meal?'

'Yes, it's this event in which two people, who like each other very much, spend time together getting to know one another more over the consumption of food, deliciously prepared by someone else.' He laughed at the face she pulled. 'I want to do this right, Bella. And neither of us want to rush into anything and I've been given the name of a well-respected babysitter who could look after the kids for us and put them to bed.'

'Who?'

'You know Verity, the lady that owns the local cheesecake shop? She's dealing with cancer at the moment, remember, from the team meeting?'

'Mmm-hmm.'

'It's her niece. She's twenty, looking to earn some extra pennies whilst she's on break from uni.'

'What's she studying?'

'I think Lorna said she was studying Economics.'

'How does Lorna know a babysitter?'

'She knows Verity and they talk a lot, from what I understand.' He tilted his head to one side. 'That's a lot of questions and not an answer. Are you stalling because you don't want to go, or is something else worrying you?'

'Of course I'd love to go! I'm just nervous, that's all. Starting something, the two of us. This part's all exciting, it's brand new and exciting, but what about afterwards? When it gets more complicated?'

He held her face gently in both hands. 'We take this one day at a time. We're not rushing. We're getting to know one another. Taking it slow. But I'd dearly love to spend some more alone time with you, without having to worry about the kids.'

She nodded. 'Me too.' It was nerve-wracking. Exposing herself to possible hurt again, but she had very strong feelings for Max already. How would she feel if she just kept trying to ignore them? That would hurt, too. 'Okay. When?'

'Probably a school night. How about I invite Ewan over to ours for a sleepover? I've got an air mattress he can use, or he can sleep in the lounge on a pull-out sofa bed. In the morning, we meet for our walk into school as normal. Neither of us stays out too late, we don't get carried away and no one turns into a pumpkin.'

'Great! Let's do it. Where shall we go?'

'Jasper's is meant to be good and that way it's in the village and we're close if either of us has to rush back for the kids or something.'

Bella smiled. 'You've thought this through!'

'I'm very thorough when it comes to planning.'

'I'm very impressed. How good are you at gardening?'

'I know my way around a rose or two.'

'Great. Want to help me uproot a lily?'

Bella sat nervously in the waiting room. It always felt strange to be the patient. Sitting out here, with all the other patients. She'd brought a book to read, in case of a long wait, but she couldn't concentrate. She'd woken with a slight headache today but she put that down to the stress of the appointment.

She'd told Max about it. Told him that she wouldn't be at work that afternoon, as she was seeing a neurologist for her headaches, but that she'd see him that evening for their dinner date and tell him all about it. But that he wasn't to worry. She wasn't. Which was a slight fib, because she was always going to worry until she got the all-clear and the professor diagnosed her with migraines.

He'd been worried, bless him. Of course he had. But she hoped she'd put his mind at rest.

And they'd had a great afternoon in the garden, pulling out that lily and then pottering about doing little jobs together and she'd felt right at home with him. Doing things like that together. She could almost pretend they were a real family. The kids inside watching cartoons whilst Mum and Dad got some jobs about the house done…

The afternoon ranked right up there with one of the best ones that she'd had. For something simple like that. She didn't need expensive dinners, or posh cars or expensive holidays. Bella just wanted to enjoy the simple things in life. And there was something special about beginnings. The excitement. The hope. The trepidation of what might be. What this might evolve into. Something grand? Something long-lasting? Was she with the guy who would become the love of her life? She tried not to think that way, but she was a romantic at heart and couldn't help herself.

Max was a good contender, that was for sure.

He seemed honest. Kind. True. She knew about his life already and there was nothing there that he was hiding. Nothing that would creep out of the woodwork at a later date to ruin everything. No ex-wives. No ex-girlfriends that still had issues with him. No weird behaviour. He was a straightforward guy. Open. Everything laid out on the table for her to view and assess.

He'd told her—'*My life is an open book. Ask me anything.*'

She'd appreciated the gesture. Appreciated that he understood her fears and that he wanted to be as open with her as he possibly could. They'd talked about Anna. Blake. The kids. Their job. They'd talked of future aspirations and dreams and he really was on the same page as her.

They both wanted happiness and security and love. The possibility of one day having more children.

It didn't seem too much to ask.

He'd put his head around the door of her consultation room before she'd left. Wished her the best. She'd thanked him. Told him she'd see him tonight and that she promised she would tell him everything that happened. Best to be as honest with him as he was being with her. The headaches were no surprise. He knew she had them and he believed, the same as her, that it was most likely migraines. They were common, even if they were a pain, but she'd told him that as soon as she had any details, she would let him know, because she understood his fears, too.

Bella put her book away. It was useless. She kept reading the same paragraph over and over again. It looked as though she was one of the only patients to have arrived without someone accompanying her. Max was at work with everyone else and, anyway, it was fine. She wasn't afraid of coming to see a doctor.

'Bella Nightingale?'

She looked over at the door and saw a nurse, holding a clipboard, who smiled at her. When she got closer, the nurse said, 'Hi, I'm Heather and I'm just going to do a short set of obs on you and take some bloods, if that's okay?'

Bella nodded. 'Fine!'

She followed Heather down a pristine corridor and into a small side room, where her observations were taken. Blood pressure, which was normal. Oxygen saturations, perfect. Pulse and respirations, normal. Blood sugar, normal. Chest and lungs, clear. Ears, clear. Then Heather took a blood sample and placed a cotton swab over the needle site and taped it into place. 'If you'd like to go back into the waiting room and Professor Helberg will call you through.'

Bella had researched Professor Helberg, of course. It made sense to, if she was going to place her trust in him. He specialised in treating patients with headaches, all types of migraines, especially hemiplegic, as well as movement disorders and Parkinson's. He had a ninety-eight per cent approval rating on the Internet, with lots of five-star reviews from previous patients. He was pleasant. Kind. Gave clear explanations about diagnoses and what next steps to take. He was happy to consult with other professionals and gave patients great confidence in his ability.

In short, the kind of doctor she was more than happy to see.

Bella was happy that all her obs had been normal. It boded well. And she felt confident when her name got called again and she went into the professor's consulting room. She shook hands with him, said hello and sat down.

Professor Helberg smiled a warm, friendly smile. 'Good afternoon. It's *Dr* Nightingale, isn't it?'

'Yes. I'm a GP in Clearbrook.'

'Ah! I was going to choose general practice one time of day, until neurology grabbed my fascination.'

'Really?'

'Oh, yes. Now then, let's see.' He tapped away at his keyboard. 'I've received a letter from your own GP that states you've been suffering from some intense headaches of late. Now, he's given me details, but I'd like to hear all about it in your own words, if you don't mind?'

'Of course. Well, they started about six months ago, to be honest. I've had headaches before, but nothing that's required me to take painkillers, they've mainly been just from tiredness or dehydration and a quick guzzle of water usually sorted them out, but in the last half-year or so

I've noticed these more intense headaches. I've been keeping a diary, to see if there's some sort of trigger—either emotional, hormonal, physical or food-based—but I can't seem to find a pattern or anything I can point my finger at.'

'And do these headaches always require pain-killers?'

She nodded. 'Yes.'

'And how would you describe them? Are they always in the same place, for example?'

'Yes. Always here, just above my eyes.' She pointed to the spot.

'And what sort of pain is it? Burning? Stabbing? Sharp?'

'All of those.'

'And do you get any other symptoms with them? An aura? Nausea?'

'I feel nauseated sometimes. Tired.'

'Ever been sick?'

She nodded. 'Once.'

'Did it make you feel better?'

'No.'

'And you've not noticed any weakness with these headaches? Nothing one-sided? No muscle weakness or difficulty with the limbs?'

'No.'

'All right. Well, I'd like to do a brief physical assessment, if that's all right with you? I'll call my nurse in to chaperone. I just want to test your reflexes and run through some neuro obs.'

'That's fine.'

'If you'd like to hop up onto the bed, I'll fetch Heather.'

'Okay.'

The professor worked his way through a standard set of neuro observations, including checking her pupillary response to light, using a hammer to check her reflexes, which would help identify any abnormalities of her nervous system. He checked her motor skills, her coordination and balance, but everything seemed pretty standard, as far as Bella could see.

'And remind me, you've not had any recent head injury? Even something small?'

'No.'

'No falls, or anything like that?'

'No.'

'No loss of consciousness with your headaches?'

'No.'

'And you don't seem to have any shaking or tremors, which is all good. No numbness or tingling in any of your extremities?'

'I don't think so, but I'm very busy, so I might not always notice.'

'Hmm. And no history of stroke, or TIAs or seizures?'

'No and nothing like that in my family.'

'And you're not taking any medications or herbs or other supplements?'

'I take a vitamin supplement. Just a standard one.'

'And everything else about your health seems normal? Periods regular?'

'Yes.'

'Okay. Why don't you take a seat back over by my desk?'

Bella went to sit down.

'All of your findings seem absolutely fine and I'm happy that, from what we've covered today, I can't seem to actually find anything physically wrong with you, which is good.'

'Great!'

'But, as a doctor, you also know that that doesn't always mean that there isn't anything wrong. This could just be migraines, as I'm sure you expect, but it would be remiss of me not to make sure, so what I'd like to do is refer you for a scan, just to make sure that there's nothing going on in the brain that should alarm us.'

Bella sucked in a breath. 'Okay.' She knew what that meant. Professor Helberg was going to check for anomalies such as aneurysm, tumour or lesions.

'And it's to rule things out, as much as it is to rule things in. You're having headaches for a reason and the fact that they've become bad only in the last six months or so suggests some sort of change. Now, it could be environmental, for all we know, and nothing to worry about at all, but I think, due to their severity, that we should get a scan and just double-check. How does that sound?'

'Would that be today?'

'Yes. Or we can arrange it for another day, if you have to be somewhere?'

She checked her watch. She should still make her date with Max in plenty of time. 'No, no. That's fine.'

'Excellent. Okay. Heather will take you through to the scanning department. When you've had the scan done, go home, relax or go and do something that's fun to take your mind off it and if, when I review it, I see anything disturbing— which I honestly don't expect to find—I'll give you a call in the morning. Does that sound like a good plan to you, Dr Nightingale?'

'Call me Bella. And yes, that sounds perfect.'

'Great. I'll call you tomorrow, but, like I say, go out tonight. Have some fun. There's nothing worse than staying in fretting about these things. At this point, I'm not worried and I don't think you should be either.'

'Thank you, Professor.'

'Call me Martin.'

* * *

It had been a long time since Max had taken a woman on a date. His last date had been with Anna. Nothing spectacular. Nothing that had cost a lot of money, but one that had meant a lot to the two of them.

He'd taken Anna to the beach. She'd wanted to watch a sunrise and so he'd figured out all the logistics himself. Picking a beach that had sand, rather than stones. Checking the meteorological websites to make sure the skies would be clear and what the sunrise times were. When to set their alarms, so he could pack Anna and baby Rosie into the car and get to the beach in good time.

It had been a lovely morning. A summer morning, so it hadn't been cold. Rosie had stayed fast asleep in her car seat for the majority of it, not even waking when Max had lifted her from the car and taken her down to the sand, where he'd placed her on a blanket, next to her mother.

Anna, despite the warmth of the day, had been quite thin and not able to regulate her temperature very well, so she'd been bundled up in blankets and had even worn a beanie to hide her bald head. And he'd sat and held his wife and sipped at coffee from a travel mug as the bluish sky had begun to change colour to molten golds and orange.

It had been a beautiful moment watching the sunrise. Awe-inspiring. He'd never really sat and watched one before, but it had taken his breath away. To watch something so wonderful. So commonplace, really, in that it happened every single day, but he had never woken early enough to watch one. Or if he had, he'd been in a city, on his way to work and juggling traffic, his mind elsewhere.

After that, Anna had become too weak to leave the house, really. But she'd spoken of that sunrise often and had told him that, when she was finally gone, when she had breathed her last, if he ever wanted to find her, all he had to do was watch another sunrise and she would be there, in all of those glorious colours.

So, it felt strange now to be dressing up and getting ready. He hoped everything had gone okay at Bella's appointment that afternoon.

I mean, it had to, or she would have cancelled.

The babysitter was already here, downstairs watching Rosie, and Bella would be here any minute to bring Ewan across.

He felt as if he was stepping into a new world. Dating again?

He'd once thought all of that behind him, but he had a good feeling about where he and Bella were going. He felt as though he was willing to risk his heart again for her, which was a huge step for him. He was ready and he couldn't think of anyone better, who made him feel the way that he did when he was with her. He missed her when she was gone. Looked forward to seeing her every morning, without fail. She brightened his day and he hoped that he, in turn, brightened hers.

This blip with her headaches…it had to be nothing, right? If the neurologist had found anything of concern today, he would have told her and Bella would have told him and then…well, he would have had to deal with it somehow. But she'd not cancelled, so that was good news and good news was great.

He heard a knock at the door and he heard the babysitter answer it and invite Bella and Ewan in. 'Max? They're here!' she called up the stairs.

'Okay, thanks. Down in one second.' He took that second to just stand in front of the mirror. Not to check his appearance, but to look himself square in the eye and give himself a little pep talk.

I can do this.

Bella is everything I could possibly want.

Enjoy tonight.

Make something good happen.

He smiled at himself then went trotting down the stairs. He could hear the kids in the kitchen and as he reached the hallway, he turned and saw Bella standing in the doorway.

She looked breathtaking. Beautiful. Her long dark hair was swept up into some complicated twist, revealing the long, smooth curve of her neck. She wore a body-hugging dress in a cobalt blue that stopped just above the knee and the fancy black heels she wore made her legs look shapely and simply stunning.

'Wow. You look amazing.'

She turned and dazzled him with her smile as she looked him up and down. 'So do you.'

'Are you ready to go?'

She nodded, holding onto a small black clutch bag that had a fringe.

'We won't be too late,' he assured the babysitter.

'It's fine. You two go and enjoy yourselves.'

'Thanks.'

He held out his arm for Bella and walked her out to his car. Jasper's wasn't that far, to be fair, and they could have walked it, but he wasn't sure how comfortable those heels were that Bella was wearing, so it seemed the right thing to do. 'Everything okay?'

'Everything's great.'

'How'd your appointment go?'

'He didn't find anything and he's not worried. I passed all the tests and we did a scan to be on the safe side, but he told me to enjoy myself tonight, so that's what I'm doing. Let's not talk about it.'

He felt greatly reassured. 'Perfect.' He wanted to give her a night to remember.

Jasper's was a stunning building. A real look of history about it, so that he felt it must have been here for a few hundred years. It seemed to have a lot of original features, but had been adorned with modern ones, such as hanging baskets filled with overflowing flowers, and window boxes. A wide pavement in front allowed for some outdoor tables and benches and a few people sat at those enjoying a nice beer or wine.

Stepping inside, he heard the soft piano music and marvelled at the low lighting provided by wall sconces. Again, there was a mix of old and new. Original features of wooden oak beams and whitewashed walls sat adjacent to round tables with perfectly white tablecloths and bud vases filled with local lavender. Historic photos of times past adorned the walls in matching black frames and he noticed, up in the ceiling, old farming tools. A scythe. Rakes. Even a pitchfork.

'Good evening. My name is Rupert. May I help you?' A man approached them, dressed neatly all in black.

'I have a reservation for a table for two? Name's Moore.'

Rupert didn't even have to check his list. He must have had it memorised or something. 'Of course. *Dr* Moore, isn't it? We have a beautiful table for you. Follow me.'

They followed Rupert through the tables towards the rear of the restaurant, going up a couple of steps and being presented with a table by a window that overlooked a lake.

'Madam.' Rupert pulled Bella's chair out for her and waited for her to sit and when Max sat opposite her, the waiter presented them with drinks menus. 'It is an absolute pleasure to have now hosted all of the doctors from the local practice. Here's to a pleasant evening for you both. Tonight's drink special is a beautiful burgundy wine, Roja St Georges. I'll be back in a moment to take your order.'

When he'd gone, Max smiled at her. 'He seems nice. And isn't this place stunning? I'd heard good things, but never imagined it would look like this inside.'

'I think Lorna and Oliver came here. I remember her telling me one lunchtime about it and she had nothing but good things to say. She recommends the beef wellington.'

Max smiled. 'I'll keep that in mind.' He glanced out of the window at the smooth, still lake, then back to Bella. 'Beautiful view, inside and out.'

She blushed. 'I don't know what to order. It all sounds delicious.'

'Shall we go with the Roja St Georges?'

'I don't normally drink alcohol.'

'Okay, we can have soft drinks.'

'You know what? No. We should celebrate today. One glass won't hurt me.'

Rupert took their drinks order and brought them their burgundy, presenting a sample into Max's glass to taste first. Max took a sip and nodded. It was delightful. Smoky. Oak laced with hints of dark cherry. When the drinks were fully poured, Rupert presented them with food menus and disappeared again. He was the perfect host. Knowing when to stay and when to go. Knowing that people preferred to chat with each other, rather than with their server, unless he was invited into the conversation.

'I'm so glad you asked me out here tonight.'

'Me too.'

'I can't remember the last date I went on.'

He had an image of a sunrise. Of a sleeping Rosie, completely unaware of the glorious colours above her. Of how Anna had felt in his arms, all bones and angles. 'I think it's probably been a long time for the both of us.'

'True. Tell me about your best date ever.' She leaned forward, interested.

'Isn't it bad form to talk about a past connection with a current one?'

'Only if you go on about it non-stop. But I've asked and I'm interested.'

He nodded. Thinking. 'Okay. Well, I guess it was the first ever date I had with Anna.'

'What did you do?'

He laughed. 'We went tenpin bowling and I very quickly learned that she was extremely clumsy and much preferred to roll her ball into the gutter than strike a pin! It doesn't sound like much, but I don't remember laughing as hard as I did that night. She was cute and funny and she made me smile so hard, my face ached the next day and I just knew I had to see her again. What about you? What was your best date?'

'Erm…probably with Blake. We went to one of those escape-room things with a bunch of our mutual friends. I just remember that whilst everyone else was trying to solve puzzles, all I could think of was to steal glances at this man that kept trying to smile at me and I just knew, in that moment, that something special was happening. Something was being created. Forged between us. It was electric. Exciting. I've never forgotten it.' She smiled and sipped her wine, nodding appreciatively.

'When you know, you know,' he agreed.

'Absolutely.' She smiled back at him, eyes gleaming.

He was beginning to feel that he knew now. Looking at her, right at this moment in the candlelight, with the piano in the background and the delicious scent of lavender and food in the air. Something was being created now. Forged now. Just as she'd said.

And the evening had barely begun.

They chatted for a while about the menu and placed their orders and after about fifteen minutes or so, their starters arrived. Scallops for Max and a seared tuna for Bella.

'This is delicious,' she said and offered him a taste. They sampled each other's food, laughing and joking, and before they knew it, their mains arrived—a chicken saltimbocca for Bella, served on broad beans with a garlic and thyme fondant potato, with a chicken jus, whereas Max had ordered the dry-aged sirloin, served with a celeriac purée, roasted baby potatoes, salsa verde and samphire.

'How's Rosie doing now? I remember how shy and uncertain she was on her very first day. Is she enjoying school much better?'

'Absolutely. She loves it. In fact, I think she prefers being at school than at home!' He laughed. 'I think because Ewan and all her friends are there, whereas at home it's just me and, let's face it, I'm not as fun as those other guys.'

'It's great that she's gained so much confidence.'

'I'm a very proud dad. She got a handwriting certificate the other day. Did I tell you?'

'No. That's amazing! Maybe we should get handwriting certificates?' Bella laughed.

'Probably!'

'Or perhaps we should get star charts? That might be fun.'

'What would we get stars for?' Max asked.

'Hmm…' She seemed to really think about it. 'Injecting babies without making them cry? Getting through the day without crying ourselves?'

He nodded. 'I don't think I'd get many stars.'

'I do think there's a website, though, for people to rate their doctors. Have you ever looked at that? Checked out your reviews?'

'I don't think I've ever been anywhere long enough for people to remember my name.'

'Well, you have. I've looked.'

'Really? What did it say?'

'That you're amazing. Kind. Helpful. That you listen well and are thorough. And one person wrote that you were sexy.'

Okay. He wasn't sure how he felt about patients saying that about him, though he knew that some patients could form affections for their care givers. For people seemingly in authority who could take care of them. He winked. 'Thanks for writing that. What do yours say?'

Bella laughed. 'Well, no one's called me sexy, but one did say that I had nice warm hands.'

He reached for her hand then. Impulsively. Framed it with his own, as if judging them for himself. He made a big show of it. Made humming noises. Turned her hands this way, then that. 'Okay. I agree with that one hundred per cent.'

She laughed and her cheeks were pink with delight.

And he didn't want to let go of her hand. It felt so good in his own. Smaller than his. Her fingernails painted a soft, shell pink. Her middle finger adorned with a gold ring, with a small blue stone. A sapphire? Topaz? Tanzanite?

His gaze met hers. 'I'm very glad that we're doing this.'

'So am I,' she said softly.

'I'd better let go, so you can eat your food,' he joked and released her hand, shaking his head at how quickly he was falling for this woman. They were meant to be taking it slow. To be enjoying each delicious moment. But all his mind wanted to do was run away with all these crazy images of what could be in the future for them.

He imagined waking up with her, going downstairs and their two kids in the kitchen eating breakfast together, a little yappy dog around their feet, as sunshine streamed in through the windows as they enjoyed being the perfect, happy, blended family.

He would scare her off with all of that. It scared him and yet he yearned for it. He'd thought that he was building a family and a future once before, but then fate had cruelly pulled the rug from under him. He'd made plans and life had laughed at him.

He needed to move much slower this time.

'Is everything to your satisfaction?' Rupert had arrived at their table.

'Everything's perfect.' Max smiled at Bella. Knowing that if anyone asked him about his most perfect date from now on, he'd talk about this one.

CHAPTER EIGHT

THEY HAD A lovely meal, sitting at their beautiful table in Jasper's, sharing the most delicious food. Bella had looked beautiful and all he'd wanted to do was sit opposite and gaze at her. But main courses led to desserts and after desserts there was only so long you could linger over coffees before you had to spoil the moment and get up and leave.

When they reached Field Lane, Max walked her to her door. 'I've had a wonderful time tonight. Thank you.'

She smiled up at him. 'Me too. I'm glad we had this planned so that I didn't have to sit in all evening worrying about…well, you know.'

'You'll get his call tomorrow and I bet everything's fine.'

She nodded. 'I'm sure it will be.' She glanced at her cottage, turned back to look at him, smiling. 'You know…with Ewan at yours, we don't have to say goodnight just yet. I don't know about you, but I'm not ready for this evening to end.'

He didn't want it to end either. 'Nor me.'

'Want to come in for a bit?'

'I'd like that very much,' he said, feeling his blood begin to race.

'Good.' She unlocked the door, stepping back to invite him in, closing it softly behind him and placing her bag on the hall table. Then she looked at him, her eyes full of longing and desire, and he couldn't resist.

Instantly, they were kissing, searching, grasping at each other's clothes, gasping, moaning as he pushed her back against the wall and held her hands above her head as his lips found her throat and his hard body pressed against her soft, pliant one.

He wanted to consume her and be consumed by her. Her taste, her scent, was driving him wild and he found the clasps of her dress and pulled them free, groaning with delight as his hands found her skin, her waist, her hips, her breasts, wrapped in slips of silk and lace.

Scooping her up into his arms, he began to carry her up the stairs, towards the bedrooms. She laughed and laid her head against his chest as he located her bedroom, where he laid her down on the bedspread and stood there for a moment, gazing at her, his desire for her almost bursting from his trousers as he undid the button, the zip, to release the pressure. She got to her knees and helped him unbutton his shirt and then his clothes were being tossed to the floor and he pushed her back against the pillows and lost himself in her.

There was no more taking it slow. Not now. How could he? He was due back at the house. He needed to let the babysitter go, so, though he wanted more than anything to savour every moment and take his time and explore her, his need for her, her desire for him, drove him onwards. They could savour each other another time. This time was for something else. Something passionate and powerful and animalistic.

He bit, he licked, he kissed, he stroked. His hands found the most intimate part of her and she was wet and slick and when he touched her there, she arched against him and groaned in the most delicious ways, he almost lost himself.

Somehow, from somewhere, a condom was produced and he slipped it on and though he wanted to wait, though he wanted to tease and tempt and play, he simply could not. He had to have her and have her now. She was everything. Her fingers raking at his back, her lips on his neck, his jaw, his mouth, her tongue entwined with his, until they both came together in a raging, explosive moment that had them both groaning and gasping for air as he felt himself come inside her, her body tightening around him in a delicious vice that pulsed and throbbed until they both lay still and sense and logical thinking came back to the fore.

She laughed, still gasping for air, and he smiled, propping himself up on his elbow. 'Are you all right?'

'I'm more than all right.' And she kissed him again and he groaned, knowing that they couldn't stay like this, couldn't enjoy more. He was expected back at his house. He had to let Verity's niece go home.

'That was...' He couldn't find any words to explain what *that* was.

Bella laughed. 'It was.' Her gaze looked dreamy and she rolled him onto his back, so that she was above him, straddling him, and she looked perfect. Her hair all mussed up, her lipstick gone now, a wonderful glow suffusing her cheeks, and her smile? It was the most beautiful smile he had ever seen. 'I don't want you to go.'

'I don't want to go either. But I have to.'

'I know.' She slid off to one side and kissed the side of his chest before rolling over, and her hair splayed over her pillow as he got to his feet and began looking for his clothes, as he removed the spent condom and then disposed of it.

This had been more wonderful than he could

ever have predicted. What he and Bella had was special and he felt good. He felt great. He hadn't felt this way for a long time.

He shrugged on his shirt. Pulled on his trousers. Found his socks. Fastened his shoes, felt her hands trailing his back and smiled to himself as he turned to kiss her. 'You're amazing.'

'You aren't too bad yourself.'

'You know you're making it very difficult for me to leave?' he said, eyeing her in her full nakedness still, his hungry gaze running up and down her body.

'Good.'

'Wicked girl.' He winked at her, kissed her one more time and said, 'You stay there. I'll let myself out. See you tomorrow morning?'

'Bright and early.'

'Sleep well and have pleasant dreams.'

'You too.'

He finally tore himself away and made his way across the road back to his own cottage. He felt invigorated, ready to take on the world! And tomorrow? When Bella got the full all-clear from her neurologist? They would. And they'd take it on together. He had no doubt.

The future looked bright and promising.

Bella woke feeling great. For the first time in ages, she'd slept really well and she had no headache this morning. Maybe orgasms were good for stopping those? she mused, with a smile, thinking of how her dinner date with Max had ended.

He was the first guy she'd been with since Blake and she'd never believed that she would be falling hard for the next guy she slept with. Realistically, it shouldn't have been a surprise to her. She'd never been a woman who'd indulged in casual flings, or one-night stands.

Max? Was special and she woke this morning feeling hopeful for the future. Happy. Contented. And looking forward to more nights like that!

Ewan had had a great sleepover at Rosie's and when Bella and Max met again in the morning to take the kids into school, they kept giving each other secret glances. Smiling. Holding each other's hands as they walked, when the kids weren't looking, and then breaking apart whenever one of the kids looked back to say something. It felt special, their little secret. It felt powerful and positive and she'd not walked with such a bounce in her step for years. And each time their hands crept back together, their fingers entwining, it felt right and wonderful and Bella felt as though she was glowing.

Eva Watts was back in her clinic for a follow-up. The lady with low iron and a domestic abuse case. When she sat down in Bella's clinic, Bella was glad that she couldn't see any new, obvious bruising, but, as Eva had said, this week Ben was away at a training camp.

'So, you received your blood results?'

Eva nodded. 'I'm glad I wasn't pregnant.'

'But your iron was low, so have you been taking the tablets I prescribed?'

'Yes.'

'You should start feeling a lot better very quickly, if you continue to use those. How are you getting on with the contraceptive?'

'Good.'

'No side effects?'

'No.'

'And did you tell Ben you were going to start taking them?'

'I told him that they were women's vitamins, to help with my heavy periods.'

Bella nodded. 'I understand. How's everything going with the relationship?'

'Well, he's away, like I said, but after talking to you, I spoke to Lorna on the phone, who's also been amazing, by the way. It's made me think about my relationship and I, er, changed the locks on the house. He won't be able to get in, when he comes back. My name's on the deeds, so he can't say it's his place. I've packed up his stuff and put it in the garden shed out back, so he can collect it, and my brother's moved in to stay with me, so I'm not alone when he gets back.'

'Wow. Okay. I was not expecting that, but I have to say I'm happy to hear that you've felt strong enough to take action and let Ben know that how he treats you is not reasonable.'

'Well, he doesn't know yet. I haven't told him. I'm going to ring him, later. I just wanted all the door locks done and secured first.'

'How do you think he'll react?'

'Badly. But he won't do anything with my brother there. Cam's a civilian that works in the police emergency room, taking calls, so he's got connections within the force, you know? He's a big guy, same as Ben, but Ben's a coward that can only take on women, so...'

'How long can your brother stay for?'

'Long enough. I'm going to tell Ben tonight. I'm scared about it, but I know it's the best thing for me. I don't deserve to be treated as anything less than amazing.'

'Agreed. I'm so proud of you, Eva.'

'I knew what was happening. I saw all the red flags, but I just couldn't do anything about it. I felt like I needed him. He made me feel that no one else would want me, because I was useless, and I lost touch with family, who'd all been wondering what the hell was going on.'

'And you told them.'

'Yes. I was terrified, but everyone was there for me. They all wanted to help and I realised just how much I was loved and how their love came without conditions, because that's what it should be like, right? A person deserves to be loved one hundred per cent. Not only when they do or behave like someone else expects.'

'That's right.'

She spent a little while longer with Eva and then waved goodbye to bring in her next patient. She was so happy for Eva and she was right. A person deserved to be loved unconditionally. They deserved happiness. As she herself had found with Max.

Her internal phone rang. A call from Reception. 'Hello?'

'Dr Nightingale? It's Saskia on Reception. I've got the secretary of a Professor Helberg on the line, who says she needs to speak to you urgently.'

Bella instantly felt sick. Her heart began thudding in her chest and her mouth went dry. 'Put them through.'

There was a click and a pause and then a woman's voice. 'Dr Nightingale?'

'Yes.'

'Can you just confirm your date of birth and first line of your address for me?'

She did so.

'Thank you. I'm Rebecca and I'm calling on behalf of Professor Helberg. He wonders if you could possibly call in today at all.'

'Call in? Does he have my scan results?'

'I don't know. All I've been asked is that I contact you and ask you to come in. He'd like to see you in person.'

In person.

Doctors preferred to deliver bad news in person. If her scan had been clear, she'd have received a text or a call, as he'd promised. Having to go back in meant it was something else.

Oh, my God, what is wrong with me? Why is everything going wrong now? Just as everything was starting to be perfect?

'Erm… I'm at work. I'm a GP. I've a clinic of my own.' She brought up her patient list. It was full, as expected. 'Can't he call me?'

'He'd like you to come in,' Rebecca insisted.

Clearly she didn't have any more information than that and this was important. 'Let me talk to my practice manager and my colleagues.' Lorna had an admin afternoon. Maybe she could take her patients? 'See if anyone can take my list.'

'Thanks. We'll see you later on, then.'

Bella was left holding onto the phone, staring into space. There was something wrong with her. Something the professor wanted to talk to her about in person. He'd found something in the scans. Something that was causing her headaches, but what was it?

Numbly, she got up and headed for Priti's office. Knocked.

'Come in!'

She must have looked white as a sheet, because when Priti looked up, she did a double take and then was up on her feet, closing the door behind a stunned Bella and helping her into her seat. 'Tell me.'

She explained as best she could. Saw realisation in Priti's eyes. Priti wasn't a doctor, but she understood. Knew the subtext.

'Don't worry about your clinic. I'll divide your patients up between Oliver, Lorna and Max. We'll carry the load. You go and find out what's happening.'

'Okay. Thanks. Will you do me one other favour?'

'Of course.'

'Don't tell Max where I'm going. He'll panic. Just say I've got a bad headache and I've gone home early, or something.'

'I don't like lying to my doctors, Bella.'

'Just if he asks. Please.'

'And are you sleeping?' Max asked his patient, Mrs Clara Dewberry.

'No. I'm not! Even though I feel shattered and everything aches. Is it supposed to feel this way?'

Clara had been into the surgery two days ago

to see the nurse, as she'd received a text from the surgery asking her to arrange a shingles vaccination. Even though Clara was only fifty-one, she had an auto-immune condition that required her to be vaccinated at fifty, rather than waiting until she was seventy.

'Side effects from the vaccine can feel very flu-like. But rest assured, you don't have the flu.'

'What about the fever and the shivering?'

'Unfortunately, they are expected side effects of the vaccination and they can last up to five days afterwards. The shot really wakes up your immune system, so that it can respond to this infection.'

'So you're saying I just need to push through it and then I won't have to suffer with shingles?'

'Yes, you have to push through it, but no, it doesn't mean you won't get shingles. It works similar to the Covid vaccines, in that it can't stop you from having the condition, but it should stop the complications that come with it. With shingles, there's a real risk—especially if you get shingles on the face, head or neck—of real complications. In some people it has been known to cause blindness or deafness. Others that get it elsewhere can suffer with a peripheral neuropathy that could last years, or even a lifetime. The vaccination is there to stop that from happening.'

Clara sighed. 'So just keep pushing through?'

'Take painkillers. Paracetamol every four hours and you could take ibuprofen in between to keep you topped up and stave off the fever and body aches. How's your arm feel where the injection site is?'

'Bloody painful! I can't lie on it.'

'I'm sorry to hear you're having a difficult time, but I'm afraid you're just going to have to soldier through it. Have you someone at home who can support you?'

'My husband. He works from home, so he's always there.'

'Well, that's good.'

He spent some more time reassuring Clara and eventually she left, feeling better that her symptoms were only temporary and led to a greater good. As she exited the room, Priti popped her head in. 'Max, are you able to take on a couple of extra patients? I need you to take two more.'

He checked his list. One, according to the records, was notorious for never showing up at all, so he probably had time, and the others all seemed to be coming in with considerably minor things. He just didn't want to run late picking up Rosie from school. 'Er...sure, should be fine.'

'Great. I'll give you Maxine Riker and George Potter.'

Max nodded, then frowned. 'Aren't they Bella's patients?'

'She…er…had to leave early.'

He looked up, frowning. 'Why?'

'I'm not at liberty to say.'

'Priti—'

'As my employee, I have to protect her confidentiality, Max. You know the rules,' she said quietly.

'But…' He knew it was useless and Priti was right. Though he didn't like the look on her face. Something was going on. Had Bella heard from the professor? His stomach lurched at the thought. Surely if it had been good news, Bella simply would have just come in to tell him? 'Ask Maxine and George to come in as early as they can and I'll slot them in between patients.'

'Thank you.'

When she was gone, he instinctively picked up his mobile phone and dialled Bella, hoping to find out more information. If she'd heard from the professor and gone home because the news was upsetting, then…

Had she gone back to see the professor at his clinic? Why? Further tests?

There's no need to panic just yet. Perhaps her scans were inconclusive. Sometimes they might not be all that clear if the patient moved in the scanner.

She'd been nervous. She might have fidgeted.

But what if it wasn't nerves and a blurred set of images?

What if they'd found something?

What if there was something seriously wrong with her?

Traffic had been heavy getting to the professor's clinic and when she finally arrived and got inside, she found the waiting room busy. She sat down, full of nerves, wondering what the hell was going on? What had been found? What was she dealing with?

If there's something seriously wrong...

Her first concern was for Ewan. If she was sick, if she needed to go into hospital for some sort of treatment, surgery perhaps, then who would look after her precious little boy? She supposed she could call one of her brothers, but they had their own lives and Ewan didn't actually know them all that well. They'd never been a close family.

Which left Max.

Ewan knew Max and if he had to stay round at their house, he'd have his best friend, Rosie, to play with too. But that was an incredible assumption she was making, because would Max be able to do that? She'd never asked him, or talked to him about this possibility, because she'd just assumed it would be headaches. Migraines, at the most. Nothing serious.

And Max...how would he react?

If she went into the professor's room and discovered it was something bad, something terrifying, life-threatening, then would Max want nothing to do with her? Would he run a mile in the other direction? This was his greatest fear, right? To be involved with someone who was sick again? The thought horrified her. She couldn't lose him. They'd taken their relationship to the next level. Yesterday had been...well, amazing. Yesterday, she'd felt so good. So happy. So hopeful. As if finally the world was being nice to her and that she just might get her happy ever after, but now?

Why am I being kept waiting?

She knew it couldn't be helped. All these other people here had official appointments. They were meant to be here. She'd been told she would be fitted in and, being a doctor herself, she knew that meant making a patient wait, sometimes. She didn't like it, but that was how it was. She'd not brought her book to read, so she had nothing to concentrate on...

Then she noticed the coffee table. Filled with magazines. She went to grab one, picking one randomly, knowing that she wouldn't be able to focus on anything inside it at all. Not one jot.

It appeared to be some sort of women's magazine with lots of lurid, gossipy headlines. Not her usual type of thing, but she began to flick through and her eyes were caught by the very first story: *My fiancé dumped me after my stroke!*

Drawn in, horrified, she began to read. This young woman, relatively fit and healthy, had taken ill at her local gym, falling to the ground with a splitting headache and losing consciousness. She'd woken in hospital, days later, to discover her left side didn't work very well after a cerebral stroke had left her with deficits. She'd had brain surgery to remove a large clot and been told that she'd probably not gain full function again, but that she'd be offered a full physiotherapy regime. The fiancé, a six-foot stud, with ripped abs, who earned a living as a male underwear model, had dumped her after she'd woken still slurring her words.

Bella closed the magazine and let out a tortured sigh. Why had she chosen to read that story? Why? What good had it done? All it had done was reinforce the idea that Max would leave her as soon as he found out about this. It wasn't fair. She wanted to cry. These were just meant to be migraines and if he left her...

She wiped her eyes and checked her watch. She checked her phone.

A missed call from Max.

Her heart sank. She couldn't call him back. Not yet. Not until she knew what was going on. Maybe this wouldn't be as bad as she feared. Maybe Professor Helberg just wanted to deliver the good news in person, rather than over the phone. There was a chance of that, right?

Wasn't there?

'Bella?'

She heard the dulcet tones of the professor himself and looked up. Throwing the magazine into her seat behind her, she scurried from the waiting room and followed him into his consulting room.

'Do take a seat.'

'What is it? What have you found?' She didn't need him beating around the bush. She needed to know. Right away.

Professor Helberg nodded and turned his computer screen so he could show her directly.

'Everything okay, Max?' Oliver had found him out in the practice's garden, after they'd all taken on an extra couple of patients to cover Bella's surgery.

'Not great, no.'

Oliver came level with him and passed him a mug of tea.

'Thanks.'

'A problem shared? You know…if you want to.'

He wasn't sure of what to say. What to share. He didn't even know if Bella had told either Lorna or Oliver about her headaches.

'I'm worried about Bella.'

Oliver nodded sagely. 'I guessed so. Is this about her neurology appointment?'

Max turned to look at him. He did know?

'She mentioned she'd booked that afternoon off for it. Has she had to go for a follow-up?'

'I don't know. She won't answer her phone. She could just be at home, but I don't know, because she won't answer.'

'It must be difficult for you, not knowing.'

Max groaned. 'I just… I just don't know how I've managed to find myself here all over again, Ols. I went through torment with Anna. I'm not sure I have the strength to go through something like that again.'

Oliver was quiet for a moment. 'You know I went through something similar with my wife? Jo?'

'I heard something about it, yeah.'

'She fought breast cancer, same as your wife,

Anna. We caught it early. Stage Two. We thought it would be an easy fight, you know. It hadn't spread, she'd go on chemo, maybe radiation, have a little surgery and it would all be over. Only it wasn't like that. Her body didn't cope well with the chemotherapy and it didn't seem to do anything to the tumour and we had to keep changing regimens, but eventually she was cancer free and we felt strong, you know? We celebrated and I told myself it was all over and thank God, because I couldn't go through that again. You think you won't have the strength. But you find it. You dig deep and you find it, because you love that person.'

'Are you saying I love Bella?'

'Don't you?'

He laughed. 'We were meant to be taking it slow, but…' Max sucked in a breath and thought about it. He had to admit his feelings for Bella ran very deep. Incredibly so. Was it love? Already? He couldn't resist her. He thought of her all the time. She made him happy just being in the same room. Last night had proved to him just how much he felt for her.

'You know, you watch someone you love be ravaged by a health condition or disease and you just know you'll do anything to help them feel better. It's all you can do. Be by their side and love them. It's all they need from you. A simple thing, really. You get the easiest job. They're the ones truly fighting.'

'I don't know if I can. It nearly destroyed me last time.'

'She just needs you by her side, Max. Whatever this turns out to be. She just needs your love and support. If you can't give her that, then tell her straight away, because she'll be fighting enough, without having to fight for you, too.'

'Can you do that to someone? Someone who's scared?'

'Jo offered me an out once. When it came back in her lung. Said I didn't have to stay with her, if I didn't want to go through that again. If I didn't have the strength.'

Max stared at him. 'And did you consider it? Leaving?'

Oliver looked down at the ground. 'Honestly? I thought about it. For a *microsecond*. I knew I wasn't going to, but still, a voice pulled at me, told me that if I did, I could walk away and be free of it all. All the stress. All the heartache. All the grief. That I could have a different life and I'd be a fool to not take that opportunity. I'm human. As a species we generally prefer the easier life.'

'But you stayed?'

Oliver smiled. 'I stayed.'

Max sighed.

'She has a young son and she's going to be

frightened. Decide what you can give and don't mess her about.' Oliver clamped his hand on Max's shoulder in a show of solidarity and then left him to his pondering.

Birds were singing brightly in the trees. As if they had no cares in the world at all. Perhaps they didn't.

Perhaps everything would be easier if he could just fly away and never look back.

CHAPTER NINE

BELLA MADE IT back in time to pick up Ewan from after-school club. After her consult with the professor, being stunned into shock with all the details, she had noticed the time and rushed back through heavy traffic to make it to Clearbrook Infant School.

She left her car outside her house and hurried to collect her son, her mind reeling with information, and she just couldn't think straight. She didn't remember the car journey at all. She'd driven on autopilot and it was lucky she'd made it back in one piece.

As she opened the door, she saw Max helping Rosie on with her coat.

Max.

He'd want to know where she'd been. He'd been calling her. Had left four messages on her voicemail, calmly and kindly asking her to please ring him and just let him know that she was all right.

Well, she wasn't all right and the news that she had, the diagnosis that she had, was not something she wanted to tell him over the phone. It would have to be done in person. Face to face. Knowing it could end everything that they had together.

He stood and turned. Saw her. 'Bella!' He glanced at Rosie, then at Ewan, and silently mouthed, *Are you okay?*

'Get your things, baby,' she said to Ewan.

As her son ran to get his bookbag and PE kit, Max came up to her. 'Where have you been?'

'I…er…had to go and see Professor Helberg.'

'And?'

Ewan came running up to show her a collage he'd made. A castle, made of pasta pieces and cloth, paint and glue. 'Wow! That's amazing!' She turned to Max. 'Not here. I can't talk about it here.'

He flinched and she felt her heart sink. If there was one thing that Max hadn't wanted to sign up for, it was another unwell partner. This was a man that did not want to have to sit beside another partner's bedside.

She was most likely going to lose him. Her one shot of happiness, of love, that she'd had in recent days, already threatening to fade away and disappear.

They walked the kids home, Ewan and Rosie babbling away together as usual, without a care in the world. Bella gazed at her son, marvelling at his perfect little happy face, free of frown lines, or dark circles or any kind of life worry. Because that was how childhood was meant to be. Carefree. Happy. How was he going to deal with a sick mother? Or worse than that? Her darling little boy. How could she prepare him for any of that?

She felt tears prick at her eyes and she quickly wiped them away.

'We need to talk, Bella,' he said quietly.

'I know! But not now, not in front of the kids.'

'Then when?'

'When they're in bed.'

'I can't leave Rosie alone in the house to come over to talk to you. Let me come back with you. The kids can go play in the back garden and we can have some privacy to talk.'

She looked at him. Felt her heart aching. He deserved answers, of course he did. 'All right.' But she didn't want to. Didn't want to impart the news that would destroy everything.

'Good. Rosie? We're going to go in with Ewan and his mummy for a bit. We need to talk about work.'

'Yay!' The two kids skipped ahead as they turned into Field Lane and before Bella knew it, they were back home.

It had been only a few hours since she'd left here this morning, but it felt as if so much had happened in the last few hours. Her whole life had changed. Done an abrupt one-eighty. She'd thought this was simply migraines. Migraines!

How wrong I was.

She unlocked the back door and the kids hurried into the garden, Ewan picking up a football and promising to show Rosie how to score a goal between two flowerpots.

'Bella.' Max went to her and crushed her into his arms. Just holding her. Squeezing her.

She soaked up every moment of that hug, just in case it was their last. Tears escaping from her eyes.

And then he let her go. Sat her down at the round pine table in the kitchen and asked her what had happened.

'Professor Helberg's clinic called asking me to go in and see him face to face.'

'Okay. And what did he say?'

'He had my scan results back and they found something. The reason for my headaches.' She didn't want to meet his eye. Didn't want to see the moment he would back away from her.

Max sucked in a breath and nodded. Girding himself for the truth. 'What was it?'

She thought back to that moment in the clinic. Of the professor turning his screen towards her so that she could see the scan image for herself. How her stomach had plummeted to the floor and she'd wanted to throw up right there in his office. 'It showed that I have a three-centimetre pituitary tumour.' A tumour that was growing on her pituitary gland, located in a hollow, just behind her eyes, which explained the headaches.

'Pituitary? So that means it's benign, right?'

'Most likely.' She nodded. 'Professor Helberg thinks it's the non-secreting type. He doesn't think that it's producing hormones.'

'Okay, and what's the treatment plan?'

'He's taken extra bloods and I'm booked in for a more detailed MRI scan, but, basically, he wants to operate and try to debulk it.'

'Debulk? So he doesn't think he'll be able to take the whole thing?'

She shook her head. 'It will mean future surgeries throughout my life, but he reassured me it's slow growing, so they wouldn't be all that often, but...' Her gaze went to her son in the garden, laughing and happy with Rosie. 'How do I tell Ewan his mummy's got a brain tumour?' She began to cry, but her tears weren't just for Ewan. They were for herself. For Max. For what she was about to lose. How endangered her future happiness was.

Max stared at her from the opposite side of the table and she'd never felt so far apart from him.

'Helberg said he'd go in trans-nasally. It's called an endoscopic transsphenoidal resection. Forceps go in here...' she pointed at her nose '...through the sphenoid sinus and to the tumour. I've got to go in tomorrow to have my eyes tested, too, check there's no pressure on my optic nerves.'

Max sighed. 'Okay. Well, at least we know that pituitary tumours don't usually spread. They're benign and don't grow fast, so that's good, right?'

'But he's going to have to keep going in, if he doesn't get it all. That means lifetime treatment. Lifetime monitoring and there could be complications with the surgery.' She looked at him, considering him. 'Look, I know you didn't sign up for this. Neither did I, quite frankly, but it is what it is and I need to deal with it and look after my son. I can't be looking after you too, so if you're not strong enough for this, then I'm giving you an out and I'm begging you to take it. It's not fair on you, to put you through something like this again.'

He stared at her. 'Do you want me to go?'

'It's not about what I want, but I need to concentrate on me and Ewan right now. I can't be distracted by you, if you're going to be hovering in doorways, not sure whether you're staying with me or not.'

'You think I'd leave you like this?'

She met his gaze then. 'Yes. Because I know you don't want this.'

He looked hurt, shocked. Then he looked down and away. Guilty.

It was enough. It told her all she needed to know. If she was going to have to get through this alone, then she needed a clean break from him. Not have it be long drawn out and painful. 'Maybe you and Rosie should go now. I need to spend time with Ewan.'

'But, Bella—'

'No, Max!' She got to her feet and physically pushed him away, her hands on his chest, her voice breaking as she erupted into tears. 'Don't make this any more painful than it has to be! You didn't sign up for this! You didn't sign up to look after me and I could be sick for the rest of my life! And you know what other detail came up from this? I may not be able to have another baby naturally, because the pituitary controls ovulation and without a pituitary then I'm screwed!'

She stood in front of him now, feeling rage and upset and grief that she now found herself in this position. 'And I don't have the strength to look after you right now! I can't watch you agonise over whether to step away! So just go! Go and leave me be!' And she stalked away and into the garden, wiping her eyes and forcing a smile and calling out to Rosie that her daddy was waiting for her in the house and was ready to go.

She didn't want to see him walk away.

Didn't want to have to close the door behind him as he walked out of her life.

There was too much going on already and she needed to be selfish right now.

Selfish for her and Ewan.

He hated how they'd left things. Bella had done her best to push him away, getting this look in her eyes that had practically told him she'd accepted it alread,y and she'd got up from that table and gone into the garden with Ewan, brooking no further conversation on the topic.

So, he'd called for Rosie and headed home. Feeling hurt. Called out. Betrayed. Yes, he'd said what he'd said before, but did she really think so badly of him that she honestly thought he could walk away from her now? He was hurt that she felt that about him. Maybe before, it might have been true, but that was before they'd got serious. Before she'd become an all-consuming force in his life.

He was already reeling from the diagnosis. A brain tumour. A pituitary tumour. Once he'd fed Rosie and she was sitting watching some kids' channel on television, he'd got out his tablet and begun doing some research.

Pituitary tumours meant that Bella could no longer drive, now that she'd been diagnosed. He read that surgery was the most common treatment for them. That recovery was quick, because the surgeon did not have to cut into the skull, unless a craniotomy was needed. That even though it was benign, she would still receive radiation treatment afterwards, especially if they couldn't remove the whole thing. That with the removal of her pituitary gland, she would have to take hormones for the rest of her life. That, yes, it could affect her fertility.

He did want more kids, of course he did, and he'd imagined that happening with her.

He closed the tablet and pushed it away and stared up at the ceiling.

Oliver had been right. When Bella had offered him that out, a part of him had considered it. The part of him that had been destroyed by Anna's passing. By watching her suffer. By sitting by her hospital bedside, praying each time she'd fall asleep that this wouldn't be the time where she didn't wake up. Where he'd watched expectantly for every breath that she took, praying to keep her with him for longer. Praying to keep her here for Rosie.

It had been selfish. Totally selfish and he'd recognised that selfishness towards the end and he'd felt guilty for it, the way he felt guilty now, because, sure, life would be easier if he didn't have to deal with all of this, right?

But I am dealing with it. I am a part of it.

Had she pushed him away because she felt in her heart that he wasn't strong enough? Had he already shown to her that he wasn't strong enough for this?

Max hated being on this side of the street. He hated the fact that there was a road that separated them, because he wanted to be with her, holding her, telling her it would be all right. And yes, if he was being honest, he did already feel exhausted at the prospect of having to go through something traumatic all over again, but that didn't matter. Not truly. He could push it to one side, because he knew he could be there for her. He loved her.

He just had to prove it to her.

She heard Max knocking on her door in the morning, ready for the walk to school with him and Rosie, but she refused to answer. Yesterday had been a huge day for her and she just wanted some time for herself and Ewan. She wanted to take the day for themselves, so that she could talk to him about what was going to happen. She'd already called Priti, the night before, to say she wouldn't be in and, just a minute ago, she'd left a message on the school's answerphone, to say that Ewan would not be attending that day.

She'd texted Max, too. Told him not to call round, but he was knocking anyway, and then she heard her letter box flap open. 'Bella? You there? I just want to make sure you're okay.'

Maybe he did, maybe he didn't, but she just didn't have the energy for him. She'd lain awake all night, curled around Ewan in his bed, silently crying. She didn't have the headspace to watch him walk away, because she knew, deep down, that this was not what he wanted or needed. Because this wasn't just about him and her, was it? There were Ewan and Rosie, too.

And she'd become part of Rosie's life and Rosie had come to love her and now he was going to have to explain that she was sick. Would be going into hospital. Having surgery. That she could die. Of course he wouldn't want to put his daughter through that. She'd already lost her own mother, why would Max want to let her lose anyone else?

No. It was better this way. Quicker. Easier. Less painful.

Rip off the Band-Aid.

A clean cut was better than one that was slow, blunt and horrific.

She loved them both, Max and Rosie, and in her own way she was trying to protect them, too, but most of all she was trying to protect herself. She was going to undergo a major surgical procedure that could change her life for ever and she didn't want to see them get hurt. It was too heavy a load for her to carry. She, Ewan, Max and Rosie had become a little blended unit. Ewan loved having Max in his life—that paternal figure she'd always wanted for him. Max was a good role model for her son and if she and Max were over now, would he lose that?

She heard nothing more from the letter box and assumed he had headed off to school. Ewan was still upstairs, brushing his teeth, and she planned to take him out today. Maybe to a play park. Treat him. Buy him something new and then, when they got home, she would try to tell him that Mummy was sick and would need to go into hospital soon.

Bella knew she needed to call her family and tell them the news. She'd need someone to look after Ewan whilst she was having surgery and then afterwards, hopefully, recovering. Even though they weren't all that close, she figured her brothers would help her. Maybe one of them would move in for a bit, because she'd hate to send Ewan away to somewhere strange. His life was about to be turned upside down—she didn't want him to have to go through the stress of being somewhere new.

Besides, she also wanted his routine to remain. Going to school each day, being with his friends and not always worrying about his mum. But how did you tell a four-year-old about something like this? Would he even understand what a brain tumour was? Should she leave out that scary word and just say Mummy needed to go into hospital for a bit and she'd be back soon?

Her phone beeped to announce the arrival of a text message.

It was from Max.

Hope you're okay. I'd like to talk to you. Please call me. Max x

Bella gazed at that little x on the end of his message. She knew this wasn't easy for him, either. She was about to put so many people through so much stress and she hated every moment of it. 'Ewan? Come on, honey, we need to go!'

Professor Helberg didn't want to wait. He'd got her scheduled for an eye test and a full MRI tomorrow back at his clinic and, once that was done, he'd said he wanted to get her in as quickly as possible to remove as much of the tumour as he could. Debulk it, if he couldn't remove the whole thing. Remove her pituitary gland and afterwards place her on hormones for life to replace those that the gland naturally made: thyroid-stimulating hormone, which did what it said on the tin, stimulated the thyroid to make more hormones; follicle-stimulating hormone, which affected the ovaries; luteinising hormone, which helped with ovulation; adrenocorticotrophic hormone, which told the adrenal glands to make its hormones. Plus there was antidiuretic hormone, which helped the body to regulate the balance of sodium and water in the body.

It was a busy gland and did a lot of things. Professor Helberg had described it as the body's thermostat.

Ewan's footsteps came thumping down the stairs. 'Where are we going?'

'To the park.'

'Why aren't we going to school?'

'Because Mummy asked them if I could take you out for the day and they said yes, as it was a special day.'

'But I was going to have a special day at school. They're bringing in animals. All kinds, Miss Celic said—donkeys, goats, sheep and a llama!'

Bella's heart sank. She remembered getting that letter now. She'd had to sign something giving Ewan permission to pet the animals.

Was she being selfish? Taking him away from

something he'd been looking forward to? 'Would you prefer to go to school, then?'

Ewan nodded emphatically.

He looked so happy, bless him, she just couldn't take him away from that. And keeping his routine was very important right now. Letting out a sigh, she smiled at him and said, 'Okay. Go put your uniform on, then. I'll take you in and give the school a call. I'm sure they'll be fine about me changing my mind.'

'Yay!' Ewan went hurtling back up the stairs.

Priti couldn't tell him anything, which frustrated him. He got why. She was protecting Bella's privacy, and he liked that Priti had their backs, but this was Bella and he needed to talk about what was happening.

Both Lorna and Oliver came to his room to check that he was okay, knowing what he'd gone through in the past and asking how Bella was. It made him feel ridiculous to say he didn't know, because she wouldn't let him in.

'She offered me an out, just like we talked about the other day, and then told me to take it. Said I wasn't strong enough.'

Oliver clapped him on the shoulder. Said he'd be there for him with anything he needed. Lorna said she'd call Bella, offer her love and support.

He felt jealous of the two older doctors. They

seemed like they had no problems at all. They were finding happiness a second time around. Max had thought that he'd found the same thing. But Bella had pushed him away.

Was she right to?

Could she see him better than he could see himself?

Had she pushed him away because she sensed a weakness in him? An approach in which he'd always been on the back foot?

He thought he'd given her everything, made her feel safe and secure, but maybe he hadn't done that at all. It was all about perception and hers was different from his.

Yes, this scared him. He could admit that.

Bella needed surgery for a tumour. Benign, but still. If the professor couldn't get the whole thing out, then Bella would be under his care for the rest of her life, constantly returning for multiple debulking surgeries and each surgery carried a risk. That meant him and Rosie sitting by her bedside, hoping for good news each and every time.

Could he imagine doing that?

Again?

The alternative was what? A life alone. Just him and Rosie, knowing that he wasn't strong enough for Bella? How awful he would feel, if he allowed her to push him away like this?

So this is when you show her that you're not weak. That you want to fight for her.

Because he knew his life could only be better by having her in it. Her and Ewan! And if that meant they had to go to hospital on occasion for check-ups and surgery, then he would do it, because he loved her! And he wanted—needed—her in his life.

Max glanced at the clock.

He could not go to find her. He had a full list. Again, they were seeing patients that had already pre-booked for Bella's list, sharing the names out amongst themselves. They were all pulling double duty so that patient care did not get disrupted.

He would have to wait for this evening and he would pack a lunch and sit on her doorstep with Rosie, if he had to, until she let him in.

Because he would not let her go.

Not ever.

They were meant to be. He was sure of it. Both of them having been given a second chance of happiness after going through so much trauma.

He was not going to let a three-centimetre tumour stand in his way!

Bella had felt so alone all day. Her mobile hadn't stopped ringing—Max, Lorna, Oliver, Priti, her brothers. Her dad. She'd not answered any, feeling the need to cocoon herself and shut herself away from people. She didn't know why she felt that way. Only that she somehow felt that if she withdrew, it would somehow hurt them less if something horrible happened.

So, when the time came for school to end, rather than need Ewan to go to his after-school club, she picked him up at the school gate at the normal time of three-thirty. Plus, she reasoned, it meant that she wouldn't see Max.

She appreciated that he had called more than most, but if it was only to confirm what she already felt was true—that it would be better for him to walk away and just be a friend—then why did she need to hear it? She was doing him a favour. Rosie, too. That precious little girl didn't need to be worrying about her either.

Ewan was full of the animal day exploits and wouldn't stop talking all the way home. She let him chatter about how soft the fur was on a llama, but how greasy it was on a sheep, and how he'd had to wash his hands after touching them all. He'd beamed with joy telling about how he'd fed lambs with a bottle of milk, how their greedy little mouths had chugged away at the teats and almost pulled the bottle from his hands. How he'd laughed. How he'd wrinkled his nose at the initial smell of farm animals.

It was a joy to listen to him. A joy to see his

happiness, and she didn't want to ruin it, so she let him carry on. Let him be a little boy for just a little while longer.

At home, she started to cook his dinner and whilst the vegetables were in the steamer and the potatoes were boiling, she sat him down at the kitchen table and told him that in a couple of days, she would be going into hospital.

'Why? Are you sick?'

'Just a little bit. But I don't want you to worry, because I've got an amazing doctor who is going to look after me.'

'And you'll come home?'

'I'll come home,' she said, hoping it was true. Hoping her procedure went smoothly and without complications. All surgery came with a risk, no matter how run-of-the-mill it was. But the idea that her son might be left alone, if the worst happened…it almost broke her heart.

A knock at her door made her jump. Then her letter box rattled and she heard Rosie's voice. 'Hello?'

She couldn't ignore that little girl, could she? Even though she knew that Rosie would not be standing on her doorstep alone.

Time to face reality.

Bella sucked in a deep breath and walked down the short hallway to the front door. She placed her hand on the handle, let out the breath and let it swing wide.

Rosie beamed and ran right past, finding Ewan immediately as Bella had known she would, leaving Bella to look at Max. He held a bunch of wildflowers in his hand and proffered them to her. 'Rosie picked you these.'

'Oh. They're beautiful. I must thank her.'

'Can I come in?'

She nodded and stepped back. Knowing this conversation needed to happen. Knowing that, at some point, she'd like to ask him for a favour, even if he was going to try and keep his distance from her. She wanted to ask him to still let Rosie play with Ewan. To check in on him, to keep things normal for him.

Max walked into her kitchen and turned to wait for her.

She'd never felt so nervous in all of her life. Even more so than when she'd waited in Professor Helberg's waiting room. 'How have things been at work?'

'Fine. Everyone sends their love.'

She smiled. Grateful. 'I got a lot of texts today. You must thank them for me.'

'I will. I'll do anything for you. Except one thing.'

Here it is. The thanks, but no, thanks.

'I will not walk away. I will not be accepting

your get-out clause. I am here. For you. And Ewan. But understand this. I am not here for you and Ewan as a friend, or as a neighbour, or as a colleague. I am here for you as your partner. Your lover. Your boyfriend, or whatever else you wish to call us. I am in this. One hundred per cent. I can't be anything else, so don't try to tell me that I am. I love you, Bella Nightingale, and I want to be there with you, every step of the way, no matter what.'

She stared at him. Hardly daring to breathe. Hardly daring to interrupt this moment of absolute shock and wonder and joy that she had not been expecting. 'You…mean it?'

'Of course! I'd hardly joke about it!'

'But you said that—'

'I know what I said, but that was before and I should never have said it. We were making silly wishes. And when people wish they often ask for the impossible. I never thought I could find anybody again as wonderful as you and I don't care if I'm going to have to sit by your hospital bedside. I don't care if I'm going to have to worry about you. What I care about is *you*. Being with you. Getting to *love you*. And if that means in sickness or in health, then I will still take sickness, because it will mean that I am *with you*. Getting to love you, and that's far better than not getting to love you at all. But…can we try for health, if at all possible?' He winked at her, his face beaming.

'But…you want more kids. So do I. That might be something that's off the table for me after the surgery.'

'There are many ways to make a family.'

'It's easy to say, Max.'

'And harder to go through. You think I don't know that? But I was a guy that would have ended my family, ended my chance of having Rosie, if it meant keeping the woman I loved and I can do that again. I love you, Bella, and if we struggle to have more kids, then we struggle, but I know we will find a way. Together. I just need you to believe.'

'I want to. But I'm so scared, Max.'

'I know you are, but let's be scared together.'

Bella rushed into his arms and squeezed him tightly. 'Oh, my God… I can't believe it. You're sure? You're absolutely sure?'

'One hundred per cent. We already have an amazing family. You, me, Rosie, Ewan. Anything else from hereon in is a wonderful bonus. I could never regret a thing with you.'

She gazed up into his eyes. His beautiful eyes. 'I love you.'

'And I love you.'

And he pulled her in for a kiss.

The kids, watching from the window, made 'yuck' noises and then laughed.

EPILOGUE

'Aw, these are cute!' Bella lifted the little hanger from the rack and showed the set of three pink Babygros to Max. 'Can we get these?'

He smiled. 'They're very cute. But we don't even know if we're having a girl.'

'We can get those blue ones, too. Hedge our bets.'

'Why not just wait for the ultrasound?'

'Hmm, sensible. But something tells me it's a girl.'

'Maternal instinct?'

'No, Rosie keeps calling the baby a girl and I agree with her. Besides, I'm carrying high and the heartbeat is faster and…' She smiled at the Babygros again. 'These are just so cute!'

He laughed and kissed her. 'You know you're a doctor, right? You don't have to believe in old wives' tales.'

'You know I'm pregnant, right? You're meant to indulge me.'

'I do indulge you. Didn't I rub your feet last

night? Didn't I go out and fetch you mint choc ice cream at midnight?'

'You did.' She laughed. 'All right. It's just... I'm excited, you know? I never thought this day would come and Rosie really wants a little sister, so...'

They'd been through so much together. So many scary days. The surgery had gone well to remove her tumour. Remarkably well. Professor Helberg had got it all. No need for her to go back and have further surgeries. She'd undergone some radiation, which had made her feel unwell, but she'd been so grateful for Max's presence. Watching over her. Caring for her. Holding her hand and listening to her fears. Making sure that Ewan was okay.

Max had held the fort and had never wavered. Never doubted.

He was the strongest man that she knew.

And afterwards? They'd had a little help to fall pregnant. IVF. Only needing one cycle and falling pregnant right away. It had been miraculous and Bella wanted to enjoy every minute of it.

She hung the Babygros back on the rack in the hospital shop. They would wait. Wait to see what the twenty-week scan said. Everything had been going perfectly up until now. She checked her watch. 'Nearly time. Shall we go?'

Max nodded and hand in hand they made their

way to the maternity ultrasound department. Ewan and Rosie were in school and getting on better than ever. They'd been so chuffed to learn that they would be moving in together and becoming brother and sister and had adapted to that so easily. She and Max had found a wonderful house to buy in the village and had moved out of their respective cottages on Field Lane and bought something a little more on the outskirts. They even had views of the lavender fields from their windows.

They sat and waited in the waiting room for a little while, feeling excited. Nervous. Desperate to know which colours to paint the nursery. And when they were called through, Bella clambered onto the examination bed and lay down, tucking blue paper into the top of her underwear to protect her clothes from the cold gel that was about to be applied.

'Do you want to know the sex?' the ultrasound tech asked.

'We do.' Bella clasped Max's hand and squeezed it tight. It didn't matter what sex the baby was. Not really. They already had one of each. Whatever this baby was would be a beautiful bonus.

Life was turning out perfect for them. Yes, they'd been through their hard times, but maybe they were done with those now. Now their lives were about starting something new. Something hopeful. Something wonderful. She was deeply in love. Happy. She could not ask for anything more.

'It's a girl.'

Bella beamed and gazed with love at Max. 'I knew it.'

'I love you so much,' he said.

I love you too, she mouthed and turned back to look at their daughter on the screen.

* * * * *

*If you missed the previous story in
the Cotswold Docs duet,
then check out*
Best Friend to Husband?

*And, if you enjoyed this story,
check out these other great reads from
Louisa Heaton*

Resisting the Single Dad Surgeon
A Mistletoe Marriage Reunion
Finding Forever with the Firefighter

All available now!